SECRET MARRIAGE EXPOSED!

Although the almighty Fortune clan will probably blow a gasket about us splashing more headlines about them, this was just too delicious to pass up. Looks like another skeleton has emerged from Eliza Fortune's gold-plated closet. And, according to our top-secret source, this sainted Fortune socialite has fallen off her pedestal for good this time.

Her family is still trying to live down her *last* romantic debacle—remember how the Sioux Falls airwaves were burning when Eliza caught her mayor-wannabe fiancé in bed with his campaign manager right before their wedding? Well, now it looks like history has repeated itself....

Turns out Eliza had a quickie marriage with ex-wildcatter Reese Parker six years ago that bit the dust when she supposedly caught her brand-new hubby cheating on her! This suave, self-made millionaire is a far cry from the rugged rodeo rider she once knew, but apparently he's still her dirty little secret. Though why someone would want to hide this strapping oilman is beyond *moi.*

Perhaps a spark of attraction still flickers between this feuding duo?

Dear Reader,

Welcome back to the world of the DAKOTA FORTUNES. This rich, powerful family has its share of secrets…and they all seem to be bubbling to the surface just now. Who's behind this latest batch of leaks to the press? I'm sure you have a few guesses, but you'll just have to keep reading to know for certain.

And you won't be disappointed with this month's selection. Charlene Sands's *Fortune's Vengeful Groom* is a wonderful reunion plot with a great twist. You'll love this self-made millionaire hero who wants nothing more than to show his "wife" what she missed out on when she left him. Eliza Fortune is about to get a lesson in well-planned vengeance.

Be sure to join us next month as DAKOTA FORTUNES continues with *Mistress of Fortune* by Kathie DeNosky, as Blake Fortune gets back at his brother Creed in a most imaginative way.

Happy reading,

Melissa Jeglinski

Melissa Jeglinski
Senior Editor
Silhouette Books

Please address questions and book requests to:
Silhouette Reader Service
U.S.: 3010 Walden Ave., P.O. Box 1325, Buffalo, NY 14269
Canadian: P.O. Box 609, Fort Erie, Ont. L2A 5X3

CHARLENE SANDS

FORTUNE'S VENGEFUL GROOM

Published by Silhouette Books
America's Publisher of Contemporary Romance

Special thanks and acknowledgment are given
to Charlene Sands for her contribution to the
DAKOTA FORTUNES miniseries.

To the V-alley Girls, Carol Pettis, Ellen Lacey
and Charleene Feldman, dear friends and striking women who
roll with the punches making my Tuesday mornings a real blast.
Your love, friendship and openhearted support bowl me over!

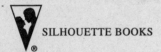 SILHOUETTE BOOKS

ISBN-13: 978-0-373-76783-0
ISBN-10:   0-373-76783-8

FORTUNE'S VENGEFUL GROOM

Visit Silhouette Books at www.eHarlequin.com

Printed in U.S.A.

Books by Charlene Sands

CHARLENE SANDS

resides in Southern California with her husband, high school sweetheart and best friend, Don. Proudly, they boast that their children, Jason and Nikki, have earned their college degrees. The "empty nesters" now have two cats that have taken over the house. Charlene loves writing both fun Harlequin Historical romances with lively characters that warm your heart and sizzling Silhouette Desire books with alpha heroes and feisty heroines. When not writing, she enjoys sunny California days, Pacific beaches and sitting down with a good book.

Charlene invites you to visit her Web site at www.charlenesands.com to enter her contests, stop by for a chat, read her blog and see what's new! E-mail her at charlenesands@hotmail.com.

THE DAKOTA FORTUNES

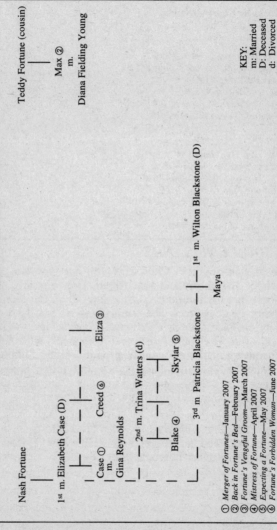

Teddy Fortune (cousin)

Max ②
m.
Diana Fielding Young

Nash Fortune

1st m. Elizabeth Case (D)

Case ①
m.
Gina Reynolds

Creed ⑥   Eliza ③

2nd m. Trina Watters (d)

Blake ④   Skylar ⑤

3rd m Patricia Blackstone   —   1st m. Wilton Blackstone (D)

Maya

① *Merger of Fortunes*—January 2007
② *Back in Fortune's Bed*—February 2007
③ *Fortune's Vengeful Groom*—March 2007
④ *Mistress of Fortune*—April 2007
⑤ *Expecting a Fortune*—May 2007
⑥ *Fortune's Forbidden Woman*—June 2007

KEY:
m: Married
D: Deceased
d: Divorced

One

"It's a stroke of brilliance, Eliza. The place looks great. Nobody does a fund-raiser like you," Nicole Appleton whispered into Eliza's ear.

From up on stage, Eliza Fortune smiled with satisfaction as her gaze traveled around the large ballroom filled with invited guests, the men dressed in authentic three-piece suits and the women in elegant gowns of the Old West. She'd designed and decorated the ballroom for the event. "Thanks, Nic. It was a labor of love."

"Well, you've outdone yourself this time. Everyone is having a wonderful time and your Basket Dinner Auction idea is going over well. You're raising thousands of dollars for the reparations to the Old West Museum."

The auctioneer announced another dinner basket to be auctioned off. Chloe McMurphy stepped up to the podium and lifted the flap on her basket, retrieving a pledge card to give to the auctioneer. "This lovely young lady will provide dinner for two, three or four. Her specialty is fried chicken and the best dumplings in Minnehaha County. And an added bonus of home-baked apple pie. Now that's what I call a real fine South Dakota meal."

Eliza tensed suddenly and glanced at her friend with apprehension. Only she and Nicole remained up on stage. All the other dinners had been auctioned off. "I hope someone bids on my basket."

"You've got to be kidding. Who wouldn't want to have a dinner cooked expressly by Eliza Fortune? At the Fortune estate, no less. I bet your dinner pledge goes for the highest bid of all."

Eliza scoffed. "Only if my father or brother decide to take pity on me. My family's out there somewhere and they know I'm not the best cook."

"Won't matter," Nicole said adamantly. "You're gonna raise a lot of money tonight—and *not* from Nash or Creed Fortune. Everyone knows how dedicated you are. They saved the best for last. And that's you."

She mouthed a silent thank-you to her friend, then took note of Mr. Phillips at the podium crooking his finger at Nicole. "Oh, look. It's your turn to go up to the podium, Nic. Good luck."

And as her friend approached the auctioneer carrying a white wicker basket adorned with a large red taffeta bow, Eliza settled back on the wooden bench seat to wait her turn.

Being a benefactor, as well as Sioux Falls Historical

Society chairwoman, she'd had no trouble convincing Siouxland's Old West Museum's president to donate some of their Western gear to help her transform a chandelier-ensconced ballroom into a springtime scene straight out of the Old West. Lariats, silver saddles and wagon wheels filled the perimeter, while bound sheaves of grain and husks of corn draped the walls. The dinner tables, though set with elegant china, rested on blue gingham tablecloths with tall, lumbering sunflowers as vibrant centerpieces. A sunrise backdrop and a large buckboard wagon filled with straw sat upon the stage just behind Eliza.

When all was said and done, Nicole's bid ranked up there with the highest so far. Her dinner pledge of roast lamb and potatoes with carrot soufflé and crème brûlée for dessert garnered over three thousand dollars. Eliza joined the group in applauding the generous bidder.

"And now, ladies and gentlemen, you have the distinct honor of bidding on Miss Eliza Fortune's dinner basket. As you all know, Miss Fortune has worked tirelessly to put on this fund-raiser and it looks like she's made it a tremendous success." Mr. Phillips reached for Eliza's hand and guided her to the podium. Eliza handed him her pledge card from her gold-trimmed basket and stood as he read her offering. "Ah, I see the winner will have a great treat in store for them. Eliza has pledged to cook any meal of your choosing, beginning with hors d'oeuvres and ending with a decadent dessert with as many courses as you desire. So let's begin the bidding at five hundred dollars."

Eliza stood smiling at her guests, while inside a tremor of apprehension coursed through her body. And only once the first bid was announced for five hundred dollars—*not* by her father or brother—did she finally relax. As the bidding continued, she grew more and more confident.

"We have a bid for thirty-five hundred dollars. Do I hear four thousand? Anyone for four thousand dollars?"

Pleased that she'd garnered a respectable sum of money, Eliza was ready to walk away from the podium. She needed to coordinate the country band's performance on stage so the dancing could begin.

"Going once, going twice for thirty-five hundred dollars and…"

"Thirty-five thousand dollars."

"I'm sorry, sir," the auctioneer said, "we already have a bid for thirty-five hundred dollars."

"I said thirty-five *thousand* dollars," a commanding voice echoed from the back of the room.

All conversation stopped in the grand ballroom, as heads turned in the direction of the voice.

Eliza stood perfectly still. Her smile faded, while her heart pounded up in her ears. She knew that voice. She would never forget the low, raspy timbre that would send her nerves spiraling out of control. She shut her eyes briefly, willing her body to calm.

It couldn't be, she told herself.

But she knew better.

She had always known that this day would eventually come.

Mr. Phillips glanced at Eliza with a baffled expression, but when she offered no help, he turned back to his task. "Uh, sorry, sorry, indeed. The bid stands at thirty-five *thousand* dollars," he emphasized. "Going once, going twice, sold to the gentleman in the back of the room!"

Just like that, Reese Parker stepped into her line of vision.

And back into her life.

After six years.

Their gazes locked from across the room. For a long moment they just stared at one another. His eyes held no warmth, his face no joy. He hardly looked like the gentle jeans-clad rodeo rider she'd met one summer in Montana.

Oh, he was as handsome as she remembered. Maybe more so now, with a chiseled jawline and dark, piercing eyes. But this man looked as though he belonged here amid South Dakota's wealthiest patrons, dressed in a dashing ink-black Western tuxedo with lines cut to perfection. A golden nugget clasped the bola tie that lassoed his neck and settled into a single-breasted brocade vest. A black felt Stetson covered shocks of short-cropped sandy hair and, as if he needed it, snakeskin boots added flair to the whole look.

Heavens, he could have stepped off the pages of *GQ*.

Eliza was aware of the hush that settled onto the crowded room. But she couldn't tear her gaze away. She simply looked at the man she had once loved.

Goose bumps erupted on her flesh.

Memories poured in, and her breath caught as myriad emotions ran havoc through her system, but the one that remained, the one she couldn't banish, washed over her like a deluge of rain.

Anger.

Mr. Phillips took his cue then and concluded the auction, asking that the bidders make good on their bids at the reception table, while the HoneyBees made their way on stage.

Eliza was grateful for the reprieve. She broke eye contact with Reese and scurried off backstage. A gentle hand grabbed her from behind, startling her.

"Eliza, where are you running off to?"

Eliza turned around, relieved to see that it was Nicole. She blinked and couldn't formulate an answer. The last few minutes had seemed like a dream. No, she corrected, a nightmare.

"That gorgeous guy bid a ton of money on you, Eliza."

Eliza couldn't fake a smile. "I know."

"And you two couldn't take your eyes off each other."

"I know that, too."

"So? Are you going to tell me who he is? You must know him. Either that or he's flirting big-time."

"No, trust me, he wasn't flirting." The very thought was absurd. She didn't know exactly why Reese had come to Sioux Falls, but she couldn't entertain any warm thoughts about him. He had nearly destroyed her with his betrayal. No one knew the whole truth, and she'd hoped to keep it that way for as long as possible.

"Who is he, Eliza?" Nicole pressed. "Please tell me."

Eliza had kept her secret for six years. Her own humiliation aside, she hated to think of the damage her revelation might do to the Fortune good name.

Good Lord, but she'd been a fool in the past. If the truth got out, Eliza would lose all credibility with her numerous charitable organizations, not to mention the headlines it would cause. One scandalized romance was enough in a girl's life. She'd managed to survive it, but this one she doubted she would ever live down.

She heaved a sigh. Keeping this from her best friend had been hardest of all. She stared into Nicole's earnest amber eyes.

"Something's going on, Lizzie," Nicole whispered, using her childhood name, reminding Eliza that she and Nicole had a long history of devoted friendship. They'd been close for more than half of Eliza's thirty-one years. Eliza had wanted to tell her countless times. She decided she'd kept her emotions bottled up long enough. Besides, if the manure were destined to hit the fan, at least she'd have an ally in Nicole.

She spoke the words she'd never said aloud to anyone in Sioux Falls, especially her family. "His name is Reese Parker and…he's my husband."

The South Dakota air made Eliza shiver, but she put up with the nighttime chill in order to catch her breath. She'd hurried out of the grand ballroom after speaking briefly with Nicole, finding this little hideaway terrace high atop the Fortune Seven Hotel to collect her thoughts. The magnificent view of the landscape had always helped put her at ease. But tonight it wasn't working.

Oh, God. Oh, God. Oh, God.

Reese was in Sioux Falls.

She doubted it was a coincidence that he'd shown up in her hometown.

I was passing through town so I thought I'd look up my...wife.

She shivered again.

And felt a wealth of warmth swarm her body as a man's jacket enveloped her shoulders. She turned quickly and came face-to-face with her husband. "Reese."

"Eliza." He stepped away from her as if he couldn't stand to be near her, yet he'd just seen to her comfort. The tuxedo jacket smelled of him, an erotic mix of musk and pine.

"You...look different," she said, fumbling for words.

"I am different," he said curtly as he removed his Stetson.

His hair was just as she remembered—thick, short and neatly groomed. How often she'd run her fingers through those locks just to muss up those perfect strands.

Eliza's heart hammered again. Even with this awkwardness, Reese held true to his manners. But he didn't look like a rugged rodeo rider right now, the man whose dimpled smile could send her body humming. There was nothing soft or gentle in the way he looked at her.

But he did look his fill, his gaze traveling over her body with a laziness that could be mistaken for arrogance. Suddenly Eliza was aware of the revealing gown she'd had designed especially for tonight. In keeping with the Western theme, the creamy satin gown dipped low in the front, the bodice forming her figure and cinching in at her thin waist. Shiny golden threads created an intricate pattern throughout and gilded wide lace teased her bosom and wrists. *To match the golden highlights in your blond hair, Eliza,* the dress designer had said.

Now, with his eyes upon her, Eliza felt exposed and vulnerable to his scrutiny. His gaze lingered on her chest, making her think back to a time when more than his eyes had devoured her.

She trembled again, and this time the night air wasn't the cause.

"It's not that cold, Eliza. Ice must be running through your veins."

Eliza had almost forgotten herself. She wouldn't let Reese get the better of her. She'd walked out on him once and she'd do it again. "What are you doing here?"

He smiled then, but not the gentle smile that softened his eyes. No, this smile was thin-lipped and hard. "We have to talk."

Eliza began shaking her head. "No. We can't. I have to get back inside."

"Tomorrow, then. During the dinner you're going to cook me."

Eliza removed his jacket and tossed it to him. "You're joking."

He caught the jacket with a nonchalance that angered her. Reese had always been fast with his hands. "I seldom joke."

But he had, years ago. They'd spent one glorious summer laughing and joking and making love. It was his quick wit and ease of manner that had attracted her to him initially. That and his hard, lean, gorgeous body.

"I can't possibly cook you dinner, Reese. I'll have someone else…"

"No. It's you or nobody." His dark eyes held hers firm.

Eliza thrust her chin up. If he wanted a battle of wills, then she'd oblige. "Then I'm afraid it'll be nobody. I have to get back inside." She turned to leave, but his hand snaked out to catch her wrist. He spun her around, and she faced narrowed eyes and a set jaw.

"You're bought and paid for, darlin'. To the tune of thirty-five thousand dollars."

Eliza's eyes widened with surprise. She'd been so distraught at seeing Reese again she'd forgotten all about the enormous donation he'd made. "You don't have that much—"

His brows shot up. "I do."

He caught her staring at the fine cut of his tuxedo, his tie clasp made of solid gold and his handcrafted snakeskin boots. She wiped the curiosity off her face, wishing he would leave. She didn't care how much money he had now. Seeing him hurt too much. She'd managed to tuck away reminders of his betrayal, but now that he was so near, all of it came rushing back with frightening force.

"Let go of me," she said breathlessly.

He released her immediately.

"I'll be over tomorrow night at eight."

She shook her head again. "It's not a good idea, Reese."

"They don't know, do they?"

He was smug enough not to have to explain. Eliza knew that he spoke of her family and the secret marriage she'd kept from them. She shook her head slowly.

"Six years, and you still haven't owned up to the truth. You must have really been…hell, never mind."

"Reese, you can't come over tomorrow night."

He scowled. "Would you rather I went to the press? News of the Fortunes was splashed all over the *Tribune* this morning. You'd think this damn charity event was the second coming or something. Wouldn't they just love to hear about the sainted Eliza Fortune's *misfortune* one summer in Montana? How she got down and dirty with a local cowboy?"

It hadn't been like that. That summer had been magical until… She drew oxygen into her lungs. "Is that a threat?"

He jammed his Stetson back on his head. "Damn straight, darlin'. I don't make them lightly."

Eliza pursed her lips to keep from lashing out. She'd lost this round with Reese. She couldn't afford for him to make good on his threat. It had taken several years to live down her last romantic debacle with a man who had aspirations of becoming Sioux Falls' youngest mayor. She'd been engaged to Warren Keyes for six months and broke off the engagement two weeks before the wedding.

Local news stations and leading headlines in the *Tribune* had kept a running tally on their breakup for weeks, and Eliza had come out the loser. Her head throbbed as she recalled the pain she'd endured finding her fiancé in bed with his campaign manager. No one knew the entire truth except her family. She'd kept quiet about his infidelity, not out of any concern for him or his campaign but because she hadn't wanted the public humiliation. Pity was the last thing she'd needed. It was bad enough that she'd suffered public scrutiny, being described as "flighty," "fickle" and "confused" when she'd walked out on him.

But what she'd really been was hurt, the injury to a young girl's heart almost too painful to bear. Warren had used her and her family's name to attain status in the community for political gain.

She'd run away then to Montana and had met Reese Parker. The ruggedly handsome cowboy had swept her off her feet. She'd fallen hard for him, and they'd had a summer affair that led to a quick wedding. Now, if the truth got out about her marriage, the term *rebound* would take on a whole new meaning.

"Dinner at eight," he said without compunction. "I doubt you remember my favorite meal, but this really isn't about food, is it?"

With that, he strode purposefully off the terrace. Eliza watched the glass door slam shut in his wake.

"Pot roast and potatoes with creamed spinach," she muttered softly.

Then trembled again.

Reese paced his penthouse suite, striding back and forth with suppressed rage. Eliza Fortune Parker, his wife, had tried to cast him off once again tonight. This time he wasn't having any of it. She'd see him on his terms, whether she liked it or not. And she hadn't liked it.

No, his appearance at her fund-raiser tonight had put a wrench in her nicely tuned life. Reese could take some satisfaction in that. He'd seen fear in her eyes, and that suited him just fine. Let her fear him and what havoc he could cause her.

She'd caused him enough grief to last a lifetime. Reese shoved his hand into his pocket, coming up with the note she'd written him six years ago, the crinkled, worn parchment he'd been given by a hotel desk clerk a constant reminder to him to succeed in life. Hell, he'd practically used the note as his bible, his guide to never give up. To never let anyone best him again.

He glanced down at the delicate writing, smudged now and bleeding blue ink.

The marriage was a mistake. I'm going home. I don't want to see you again. Ever.

Ever.

Damn her. He'd stayed away long enough.

He knew every cold, harsh word of that note by heart. It was time to end it all, and too bad if it didn't fit into Eliza's plans.

Before his father died last month, he'd made Reese promise that he'd get his affairs in order. With unspoken words, he'd immediately known what his father had meant. Normally, Cole Parker didn't pull punches. He'd been one up-front tell-it-like-it-is kind of man. But his father had known that Eliza Fortune Parker had been Reese's one weak spot so he'd trod carefully.

It's time, Reese, he'd said, almost on his last breath. *Take hold of your life, son.*

His father had been right. It was time.

But Reese would take his time, making Eliza squirm, upending her perfect little world, showing her that he wasn't the sweet-natured, bronc-busting cowboy she could tie up in knots, anymore.

God, he'd been a fool thinking that the rich, pretty socialite would be happy with a down-on-his-luck cowboy.

Reese winced and crumpled the note, shoving it back into his pocket.

Man, but he'd loved her. She'd come to Montana and he'd seen something unique in her, something beautiful in her heart. She'd turned him on with that body of hers, wearing clothes that hid her perfection. His imagination had taken wild rides, until he'd known he had to have her. And once they'd made love, it had been better than good. So damn much better than anything he'd ever experienced.

When Reese's cell phone rang, he checked the number, then smiled. "Hey, Garrett."

"Where are you, bro?"

"In the Providence Hotel."

"Top floor?"

"Penthouse." Reese could picture his brother's grin. They'd often joked that once they struck it rich, they'd never stay in anything but the best—a result of too many sleazy motels with torn sheets and rodents as bed partners.

"I take it that's not a Fortune acquisition?"

"Hell, I had to drive across town to find a decent hotel they didn't own."

"You're home early. I take it the night didn't go well?"

"On the contrary. I accomplished my goal."

"Which was?"

"You wouldn't approve, Sir Galahad."

His brother sighed. "So, how is Eliza?"

Beautiful, sexy, cold as ice. "She hasn't grown fangs or anything."

"Ah, still a knockout."

Reese didn't answer.

"Hey, I'm on your side, Reese. We're family. But I liked Eliza from the moment I met her."

"You only met her one time."

"True, but I could tell she was crazy about you. I thought you were a lucky man. And Pops, well, he wanted you to sort out your life, Reese."

"That's what I'm doing. I plan on getting her out of my life."

There was a long pause. "Are you sure that's what you want?"

Reese let out a bitter laugh. He knew his brother only meant well, but what option did a man have when his wife walked out on him without any explanation. She'd kept their marriage a secret because she'd been ashamed of him and his status in life and feared her family wouldn't approve. She didn't care enough about him to fight for what they had. He'd been broke, making his way through the rodeo circuit and pouring all of his money into his venture. But Eliza hadn't stuck around long enough to see his dream come true. When she'd had enough, she'd simply walked out. Without taking a backward glance. Well, he's making her take a good long look now.

"I'm sure."

"Okay," Garrett said quietly, and Reese knew his brother only had his welfare at heart. "Hey, want some good news?"

"Shoot."

"We had a blowout in Cinder Basin. A real gusher.

Your instincts were right on. That makes seven straight oil strikes, Reese."

Reese's mood lifted. "Pops would've liked to hear the news."

"He knows, Reese. He's overseeing our operation from up above."

"Yeah."

Reese had ridden the rodeo circuit to sustain his dream, using his winnings to help finance his venture as a wildcatter. He'd worked long and hard coming up with nothing but dry holes his first three years. The standing joke was that he couldn't find oil in a gas station. But then his luck changed and his rigs started paying off. He became a respected oilman, hitting five straight blowouts that year, and his success continued to mount every year, his ratio of blowouts to dry holes ten to one. It hadn't taken him long to form his own company—Parker Explorations being one of the most prosperous oil companies in Montana.

"Thanks for the call, Garrett. I'll be dreaming of black gold."

"You're going to need it with that house you're building."

Reese agreed. "Yeah, it's a money pit, but it'll be perfect when I'm through."

"Perfection has its drawbacks at times."

How well he knew that. At one time he'd thought he'd found the perfect woman, the perfect wife. They were to have the perfect life. Eliza had crushed that idea and left him a broken man. It had taken him a long time to dig himself out of that hole. But now he was back on top and nothing was going to stop him. He had the *perfect* plan for getting back at his wife.

"Yeah, but when you get it right, there's nothing that compares to it."

Two

"Here are the books you requested, ma'am." Ivy Woodhouse, the Fortunes' chef, handed Eliza three cookbooks as she sat in the great room just off the kitchen. "Are you sure you don't need my help for that special meal you're cooking tonight?"

Eliza glanced up at Ivy. "No, but thank you for the offer. I plan on doing this myself," she said.

Even if it kills me, she thought. She couldn't risk having the cook or anyone else around when Reese came over tonight. "In fact, since my father and Patricia won't be home this evening, why don't you take the night off."

Ivy's brows rose in surprise and she paused briefly before answering. "Thank you. Shall I set the table for you, miss?"

"I'll take care of it. Enjoy the night off, Ivy," she said as the cook thanked her again and left the room.

Eliza leaned back against the sofa, planning her dinner outside on the veranda, where no one would bother them. She remembered the chills she'd experienced last night when Reese had joined her on the hotel terrace. Most of what she'd felt had little to do with the weather. She'd been shocked and then angered by his appearance, which she believed was the exact reaction he'd wanted from her. He'd made her darn uncomfortable last night.

Now she had the chance to return the favor. If she could make Reese uncomfortable enough, maybe the evening would end quickly. She'd be willing to endure a slight frost to get rid of Reese. His presence here in Sioux Falls made her jumpy, but having him show up at her home tonight could surely do her in.

As luck would have it, her father and stepmother had dinner plans this evening. As for the rest of the family…hopefully they wouldn't make an appearance, either.

Eliza opened a cookbook and began flipping pages.

Her father took a seat in his wide velvet-tufted wing chair, facing her. "Good morning, honey."

Eliza lifted her face and smiled. "Hi, Dad."

Nash Fortune, never one to miss a sign, sent a worried look her way. "Tired today?"

"Not really," she said, telling a little fib. She'd spent a restless night worrying about what Reese's appearance in Sioux Falls might mean, and she feared the lying would only continue.

"You worked very hard last night, Eliza. The fund-raiser was a huge success. And, as a father, I couldn't be more proud of what you managed to accomplish."

"Thanks, Dad, but it wasn't all me. I had a great deal of help and—"

"And you're the one with the ideas, the guts to pull it together, to make it all work, right down to the final dotting of the *i*'s and crossing of the *t*'s. I understand you've outdone yourself this year, bringing in more money than the museum had ever hoped."

"Yes, I'm happy we raised the funds they needed for the repairs."

"The gentleman who bid on your dinner put you over the top."

Eliza slammed the cookbook closed, took a deep breath, then nodded.

"Do you know who he is? Where he's from?"

Eliza's heart raced with dread and she cursed Reese for putting her in this position. Her mind fumbled around for just the right words. "Montana, I believe. He's passing through Sioux Falls."

"Just passing through?" Her father scratched his head, then furrowed his brows in a gesture Eliza knew so well. When Nash Fortune wasn't buying something, he couldn't hide the expression on his face. His instincts were usually right on, but the man didn't have a poker face. "Why would he donate so much money if he had no stock in Sioux Falls? No one I questioned seemed to know."

Eliza clenched her teeth. Her father had asked people about Reese Parker? "It's a good tax deduction," she said, keeping her comments noncommittal, "and a wonderful cause, Dad. Maybe he's generous by nature."

He didn't seem convinced. "I suppose. Too bad I won't be meeting him tonight. Patricia's been a little down lately, so I thought a romantic dinner for two at her favorite restaurant would help lift her spirits."

"Patricia mentioned that you wouldn't be home tonight for dinner. I think she's excited about some alone time with you."

Eliza envied the love her father and Patricia shared. He was devoted to her. And after losing Elizabeth—Eliza's mother—early in life, he'd rebounded with a disastrous marriage to Trina Watters before finding true love again with Patricia. Eliza had once thought she'd found that same kind of love, but nothing with Reese had worked out as she'd hoped.

Her father glanced down at the cookbook still in her lap. "So what kind of fabulous meal are you planning for tonight?"

"Don't say *fabulous* and *meal* in the same sentence when you're talking about me. I'll be lucky if I don't poison the man."

Now, there's a thought.

Her father's lips twitched, but he didn't comment any further. Nash Fortune was a wonderful husband to his wife and a caring father to Eliza, but he never showed her much outward affection. She knew her father loved her, but he'd also held high expectations for all his children. Case, Creed and Eliza all did their best never to disappoint him. They'd wanted his approval as much as his love. But Blake and Skylar, her half brother and half sister, were a different matter.

And now, with Reese Parker on the scene, the truth of her six-year secret marriage might hurt her family, disappoint her father and splash unfavorable headlines in the newspapers about the Fortune name.

Eliza shoved that thought aside and instead focused on something else. "Was my mother a good cook?"

Her father stared off for a moment as if reliving another time in his life. When he spoke, his voice broke with a certain reverence mingled with pain. "Your mother was good at everything she did…."

Eliza listened carefully, noting the momentary winsome look on her father's face. It was an expression she'd seldom witnessed.

"Except cooking," he finished.

She released an amused sigh. "Oh, Dad, really? I take after her?"

He looked into her eyes. "She was smart and dedicated to what she believed in, pretty as a picture—and couldn't cook worth a darn. Yes, you take after her."

Eliza had heard some of these things before, but she never minded hearing them again. It made her feel closer to a mother she'd never known. She'd wanted so much to know the kind of unconditional love that she'd seen among her girlfriends with their mothers.

"I loved her dearly, Eliza. You know that."

She nodded. "I do know that."

Her father stood, then and placed a rare but much-needed kiss to her forehead. "Good. And, honey, no matter what you cook tonight, if the man is a real gentleman, he'll eat it without complaint."

* * *

"Except the man isn't a gentleman," Eliza said to Nicole over the phone hours later. "And the weather gods aren't cooperating, either. A light mist is falling. We can't eat out on the veranda as I'd hoped."

"So why not use the dining room?"

"No, I can't do that. *Family.* Patricia and my dad will be gone, but I can't chance anyone else popping into the house and overhearing our conversation. I've set everything up in my design studio. If the rain stops, then we can go out onto the veranda."

Her gaze traveled around her beloved room, where she'd spend hours dreaming up designs and wishing that one day she could open her own studio. She realized suddenly—and perhaps too late—how the room appeared. In an effort to conceal the mess, she'd arranged beautiful lengths of silk and satin cloths, draping them over bolts of fabric, design charts, spools of thread and ribbon. With soft lighting, her work area hidden and colorful material flowing in an array of delicacy, she'd unintentionally created a dining area that one might conceive as seductive.

"I think this might be a mistake, Nic," she said slowly, trying to calm her impending panic.

"You'll do fine, Lizzie. You always do. Just keep your head up, your mind on something else and you'll get through this evening."

That had always been her problem with Reese. Whenever he was in the room, she couldn't focus on anything *but* him. She'd met him right after watching the rodeo and walked up to him in a meet-'n'-greet line to shake his hand. He'd held on to her hand a little longer than the other cowboys had and looked deeply into her eyes with a certain sweet promise, then released her to shake the next person's hand. She'd been fascinated, transfixed in the moment—and disappointed when she'd left the rodeo without seeing him again.

So when he slid in the seat right next to her that night at her hotel bar, she'd been captivated by his slow and easy manner, quick wit and undeniable sex appeal. She'd fallen hard for Reese Parker, and she'd realized right then, that what she'd felt for Warren Keyes wasn't love at all. She'd dismissed her feelings for him quite easily after meeting Reese.

She'd had the real thing with Reese—or so she believed. And when he'd betrayed her, her world had crumbled apart.

"Thanks, Nic. I don't know what I'd do without you." She'd never regret telling her dear friend the truth. She'd been a godsend today, coaching her through the cooking and giving her moral support.

"So, are you wearing a knockout dress?" Nic asked.

"No, just a plain black cocktail dress with simple lines. I don't really care how I look to Reese."

Nic sighed. "Eliza," she said, taking a serious tone, "you were married to him. I mean, you're *still* married to him. A woman who's been placed in your situation would surely want the man to eat crow…at least for a little while."

"It's not crow, Nic. It's pot roast. You helped me with the recipe, remember?"

"Is that a joke coming from my worried friend? Maybe there's hope for you after all. Besides, I *know* that black dress you're talking about. And it's killer on you. You could make a burlap sack look great with your figure."

Eliza closed her eyes briefly, wondering if Nicole had a point. After all, why had she chosen Reese's favorite meal to serve unless a small part of her wanted him to see what he'd missed out on these past years. A small part of her wanted him to recognize that he'd thrown away an abiding love. Maybe she had chosen a dress, though conservative in design with a high neckline and a decent hemline, that seemed to set off her curves. With Eliza's body, unless she truly did choose a sack to wear, she could hardly conceal her womanly form.

When the doorbell rang, she froze. I need more time, she thought. I'm not ready for this. "He's here," she breathed into the phone.

"Eliza, keep your cool. Be honest with him. And whatever you do, don't…"

"What, Nic? Don't what?"

"Don't fall for the guy again."

"Not a chance. I'm immune to his charm now. I've learned my lesson with Reese Parker."

She clung dearly to those thoughts as she descended the stairs and greeted her estranged husband.

Reese Parker stood outside the Fortune estate, barely containing his temper. The last time he'd been here, he'd been effectively tossed off the property. Now he was an invited guest. Hell, not exactly. It had cost him to get this invitation, but it would be well worth the money paid to see Eliza's reaction when she learned the truth about him. She'd toyed with his affections in the past, then cast him aside. Reese would only give her a dose of her own medicine.

He rang the doorbell, and when the door opened, he was surprised to find a nervous Eliza standing there instead of one of the staff. "Still keeping secrets, darlin'?"

Her chin jutted up, angling her nose in the air, but she couldn't conceal the rosy color flaming her cheeks. "I thought we could be civil to one another tonight."

Think again, he wanted to say, but she did have a point. Nothing would get settled if they couldn't stand to look at each other all evening.

Although looking at Eliza had never been his problem. She'd captured his attention from the moment they'd met. Tonight, she dressed in a classy black dress that attempted to hide a body he'd tried damn hard to forget. With blond hair caressing her shoulders and those soft blue eyes—glaring at him right now—Reese remembered her all too well, *in* and *out* of her clothes.

He stepped inside and handed her a bottle of Dom Pérignon.

A faint smile crossed her lips when she glanced at the bottle he'd given her.

When I make my first million, we'll celebrate with Dom Pérignon.

Reese had always wanted the best for her, no matter the cost, and now that he could afford it, he knew the champagne would taste bitter to them both.

"I keep my promises," he said quietly.

Eliza nearly dropped the bottle she held. "Except the most important promise of all," she said, handing him back the champagne. "Dinner is waiting."

Reese set the bottle down on an entry table and arched his brows. He hadn't really wanted to drink champagne with her. No, his intention was to make a point, and he wasn't entirely sure he'd succeeded.

Eliza led him up a wide winding staircase to the second floor. It irritated him to no end the pains she took in order to keep their marriage a secret. She'd probably arranged for the entire family, as well as the staff, to be gone this evening. Fine by him. He wasn't overly fond of the Fortunes anyway, from the little Eliza had shared with him about her family. And now she was tucking them both away somewhere on the second floor.

"You have a dining room up here?"

Eliza rolled her eyes. "We need privacy. We'll dine in my studio."

"Ah, worried that your father or brother might stumble upon the domestic scene? Wonder what they'd say to see you actually dining with your husband?"

"Shhh. Please, Reese. Keep your voice down."

Reese clammed up, but not to ease her distress. His plan of action called for charm and wit, not anger. He'd had six years to stew and now he'd have to control his boiling point.

He followed her into a large room that appeared welcoming and warm, a room that clearly wasn't ordinarily used for dining. Yet she had a table set beautifully with all the finery he'd have expected from a Fortune and she'd obviously gone to some trouble to conceal a work area using drapes of material. Reese felt himself relaxing some. "This is nice."

Eliza shut the door behind them, then let out a deep sigh of relief. "We can talk in here without…"

Reese raised his brows. "Without?"

"Interruption. Would you like to have a seat?"

So formal, he thought. Had she forgotten how it'd been with them? The laughter, the sweet promises, making love anywhere and everywhere, including the backseat of his truck. Reese shoved aside an image of Eliza straddling him on a chair not too unlike the one she so properly offered him just now. She'd been beautifully naked, gripping him tight and rocking that chair for all it was worth.

He removed his jacket and loosened his tie.

Eliza approached, coming up close enough for him to catch a whiff of her scent. The familiar exotic perfume teased his nostrils, bringing back even more memories. She still wore the same fragrance that had lingered on his clothes for weeks after she'd gone.

"I'll take that," she said, reaching for his suit coat.

He handed her the jacket and sat down. Within a few moments, she joined him at the small round table. When she uncovered the dishes, he glanced down at the meal, then lifted his gaze back up to her. "Pot roast and all the fixings."

"Yes," she said, meeting his eyes as though meeting some sort of challenge, as well.

Reese studied her for a second, while something fierce slammed into his gut. She remembered. Damn her. They'd had a good thing, and she'd destroyed it—and him, nearly—when she'd walked out of their marriage. Well, he was here to set things straight. He tempered his anger with the knowledge that he would do just that. Then he'd be gone.

Reese took a bite of the roast and nodded. "This is very good."

Eliza's lips trembled into a little smile. "Thank you. I, uh…my cooking ability hasn't improved much, but I'm happy with the results."

Reese swallowed and leaned back in his seat. "Are you saying you cooked this meal?"

She nodded. "It was a huge donation, Reese."

"So you figured you owed me? You figured—"

"I'd do the same for anyone who made a bid," she said in a rushed breath. "It's only right."

Too bad his wife had a slanted view of what was right or not. She'd honored her pledge to cook a meal for a hefty donation, but she hadn't the decency to tell him to his face that she'd missed the good life and was leaving him high and dry six years ago. Reese let her comment drop for the time being.

He scanned the room again, this time with discerning eyes, noting the objects partially hidden behind draped fabrics. "So what is this place?"

Eliza's eyes brightened for the first time tonight. "It's my studio. I do interior design. It's something I've always enjoyed."

"Are you in business?"

She shook her head. "No. Maybe someday," she said on a wistful note. "I've decorated the third floor of the estate. And I use my talent for charitable events at times."

Reese forked another mouthful and chewed thoughtfully, wondering about Eliza's life. Didn't sound as though she lived on the edge anymore. The Eliza he'd known had been part risk taker, part sexy bed partner. She'd been carefree and happy—or so he had thought until he'd realized that he had been her entertainment that one summer.

Now she spent her time raising money for good causes, but it seemed, from the light that sparked in her eyes just then, that she wasn't pursuing her true passion. He'd noted the longing on her face when she'd let down her guard.

He glanced at her full plate. "Not hungry?"

She lifted a quick smile to him and picked up her fork, ready to stab the meat. Then she lowered the fork down none too gently. "Reese, why'd you make such a large donation last night?"

He smiled. "Because I can."

Eliza's blue gaze met his. He'd always thought she had the prettiest eyes. That hadn't changed, only now he knew what kind of deceit those eyes could conceal.

"How can you? What's changed in your life?"

"I told you one day I'd strike oil, darlin'."

She slumped back in her seat, stunned. "You mean… you did it? You actually… I never thought…"

"That was the problem, wasn't it? You never believed in me. You never thought I'd fulfill my dream. All you saw was a silver-buckled rodeo cowboy without a dime in his pocket." His tone turned gruff. "But after you left, I made it my mission in life. I partnered up with my brother Garrett. We pooled our resources. With his business sense and my gut instincts we struck oil after two years. Now Parker Explorations is a successful wildcatting company in Montana."

"You own your own company?"

Judging by the look of awe on her face, she appeared truly surprised. Reese had wanted that reaction from her, but now it seemed that her lack of faith in him achieving his goals just irritated him even more. He'd wanted to shock her and rub his success in her face to gain well-deserved satisfaction. He'd done all that, but it wasn't enough, damn it. "Let me get this straight. You married a rodeo cowboy from Montana and never in your wildest dreams did you think I'd amount to anything. I had no money, and that just wasn't good enough for you. After our little summer fling, you got tired of playing the penniless wife and headed for home. I get that now. But you should have stuck around. My company is one of the fastest growing in Montana, and now I'm finally setting down roots. I'm staying in one place for a change and building my own estate just outside of Bozeman. So let's just call our marriage what it really was—a foolish notion. Or how did you say it in your note? *A mistake.*"

Eliza blinked, then stared at him as if he'd gone raving mad. "Reese! What are you talking about? I didn't run out on you because of *money.* And I certainly wouldn't have married you if I hadn't lo—"

"Hadn't what, Eliza?" he probed, shoving his plate away and leaning in with elbows braced on the table.

She hesitated for a moment and then on a long-winded sigh finished, "Hadn't thought it would last forever. I'd planned on staying married, but you…you were the one who made that impossible. How could you think I'd stay in a marriage to a man who'd been unfaithful? After less than three months together, Reese! I'd trusted you. And you, you…"

Reese tossed his napkin onto the table and bolted out of his seat. "What?"

"Don't pretend you don't know what I'm talking about."

"I *don't* know what you're talking about! I was never unfaithful."

Eliza sat perfectly still in her seat and spoke slowly. "I'm not a fool, Reese. But apparently you thought I was. That last night, when I left you to go home for my father's surprise birthday party, I came back to our hotel room unexpectedly and saw her."

Completely baffled, he asked, "Saw…*who?*"

"The rodeo queen. Suzette, SueBelle, Sue…something. She was in our bed. *Our bed!*"

Reese slumped back into his chair as faded memories came back and he recalled that night. He'd kissed Eliza goodbye in front of the hotel, hoping she'd go home and finally have the courage to tell her family about him and their marriage. He'd met up with a friend from the rodeo named Cody Pierce and together they'd gone to the bar for a drink. Aside from missing his wife already, he'd had an event that next day so he'd decided one drink would have to be it. "Her name was Susanna."

Eliza nodded scornfully. "So you don't deny it?"

"Damn straight, I deny it. I never touched that woman. No, that's not true. I did touch her…."

Eliza's expression blackened.

He was so damn angry with her right now that he didn't give a damn what she thought, but he hated being accused of something falsely. "I was at the bar with Cody that night. You remember him. He's the big, good-looking bull rider who always managed to flirt with you."

Eliza opened her mouth to respond but clamped her lips together, apparently deciding against it.

"We spotted Susanna in the corner, drinking herself into oblivion. She was really wasted. It seemed her younger brother had gotten in a bad car wreck and she couldn't catch a flight out of town until the morning. She was pretty upset and then announced that she'd drive herself all the way to Texas if she had to. When she stood up to leave, she would have collapsed if Cody hadn't caught her. We both knew if we left her, she'd do something stupid. Since you were gone anyway, we put her in my bed, talked to her awhile and waited until she fell asleep. I bunked with Cody that night."

"Sounds like a good story," Eliza said bitterly, "except when I entered the room, she called out your name."

"And did I go to her? Did you see me? Hell, no. Because I wasn't there. It was after midnight when we finally got her to sleep. And when I went to check on her just after dawn the next day, she was already gone. She couldn't have spent more than a few hours in our room. I was never alone with her."

"But…but I thought… I came back so unexpectedly, and when I saw her…I assumed—"

"I know what you assumed," Reese said, barely managing to contain his hurt and anger. He'd given Eliza everything he had to give, but still she hadn't trusted in him. She'd instantly thought the worst, without even bothering to stay and confront him to get to the truth. "Did you really think I'd be unfaithful to you? Where were you for those three months we had together? Didn't you know how I felt about you?"

Eliza closed her eyes slowly, her face void of expression.

"What brought you back that night, anyway?"

She opened her eyes, the pretty blue tarnished with regret. "My…my father took ill. It was nothing serious, but Patricia decided to postpone the party. And I was so happy to come home to you that night that I rushed inside that room and then…saw her there."

"So you wrote me a note."

She stiffened and then sank her hand into her hair. "Yes. But first I ran. I couldn't help it. I had to get away. I came back just before dawn after crying my eyes out in my car. I decided to leave the note with the front desk clerk."

"Why? Why not blast me right then and there if you thought I'd been unfaithful? At least the truth would have come out. And we wouldn't have wasted six years of our lives."

"I couldn't," she said, the regret in her eyes turning to pain. "I couldn't because… You know that I had a broken engagement right before I met you."

"Yeah, that's about all I know. You never gave me details."

"You didn't seem to want any."

"What for? I only knew that I wanted you. I didn't care that some loser let you go."

"But you see, it's so much more than that. He hurt me in ways that I can't describe. And then when I thought you had betrayed me, too...I couldn't face it. Or you. And I couldn't face another disastrous scandal. I'd put my family through enough that year, breaking off that engagement. The headlines were cruel and probing...and I just couldn't put my family through that again."

"So you walked?"

She nodded.

"And it never occurred to you that I might have been innocent?"

Eliza lifted her eyes to meet his squarely. She breathed out, "Not once."

"Not once," he repeated. He tamped down rising rage. *Not once* had she even thought it possible that what she'd seen had been something harmless, something that could have been easily explained if she'd only sought the answers.

She continued in a quiet tone, "It was like I was reliving a scene from my past. First Warren's betrayal, then yours. We'd been engaged for months, and two weeks before our wedding date I found him in bed with his campaign manager. He hadn't expected me to show up when I did, either. But when I caught him, I realized that he'd used me and the powerful Fortune name for his campaign. He wanted to be Sioux Falls' youngest mayor. I guess I never really got over that betrayal."

"So you thought I was just like him?"

"No…yes. I don't know," she said, tears misting in her eyes.

"I never asked you for anything. In fact, I refused your money time and again. That's not what I wanted from you. I only asked that you love me. But you didn't. Maybe you weren't ready to get married, Eliza. Maybe you still loved this guy and only used me to get over him."

"No! That's not true." She rose from her seat and implored him with fire in her eyes. "I didn't love Warren. Not the way I loved you. He got what was coming to him when he lost the election, and I knew a moment of satisfaction in that. But it all seemed so trivial to me because when I met you, I fell in love and didn't care a thing about Warren anymore. I never thought of him that way again."

"Except the moment there was a hint of doubt about me, you cast that so-called love aside. No, Eliza. I'm not buying it. That's not what love is about."

Eliza's indignant expression faltered.

Reese hadn't expected this. No, he'd always thought she'd walked out on him because he couldn't provide the money and lifestyle she'd been accustomed to. They'd spend their days traveling the rodeo circuit, spending their nights often in a different motel room, in a different city. He'd been so sure that she'd gotten tired of the instability and the lack of luxury.

Now he was blown away by her allegation. She'd really believed that he'd deceived her and he'd had an affair the minute her back had been turned. This truth was a fresh injury to an old wound, one he'd nursed through the years until he'd thought it healed. Now she'd opened that old scar up and plunged it deep with a new sharp and gutting accusation.

Even now, as he gazed into her solemn eyes, he read doubt and mistrust there. What did it matter that she didn't believe him? After all, he hadn't come here expecting a happy reunion.

"What now?" she asked, and he noted worry on her sullen face. She didn't want their marriage exposed; that much was evident.

He approached her, his gaze holding hers. Eliza backed away from him and he smiled. And the more she backed away, the closer he came, until she bumped into a worktable draped with white satin. He grabbed her hand and drew her near, while the other hand reached up to caress her face. She stared at him. He skimmed a finger down her cheek, tracing the delicate lines. Her skin felt smooth and utterly soft, just as he remembered. He skimmed his hand farther down, grazing her throat and then stroked lower to flatten onto her collarbone.

She drew in a quick breath, the gasp reminiscent of the passion they once shared. Heat was still there between them, simmering from their bodies. And want was still there, too. Her pulse pounded under his palm.

He slid his hand to her breast, spreading out to cup her fully. Even through his anger and hurt, the remembered feel of her created havoc below his waist.

He flicked his thumb over her pebbled nipple.

She made a sound in her throat, a little cry that drew him to full erection.

He leaned in, pressing her body to his, his mouth angling toward hers. "Now, darlin', I give you something to worry about."

Three

If she pushed at him, she knew he'd release her and back away. But Reese's heat surrounded her. His eyes held her captive. And those lips, hovering so near, tempted her beyond reason. Eliza's body responded to his.

It always had.

So when he freed her breast and splayed both hands around her waist, tugging her closer, she allowed it. And sighed when his erection rubbed into her belly.

Her mind flashed images of making love with Reese in all ways and all positions imaginable. They'd been hot for each other. They'd never let up.

They'd been madly in love.

"Kiss me, Eliza."

And there it was—the low timbre of Reese's command. He'd always brought her pleasure. He'd been an incredible lover, a man who spoke to her in bed, telling her what he wanted and what he would do to her.

He'd been sinfully erotic, sexier than a man had a right to be. He'd brought her fulfillment each and every time.

Yes, yes. She wanted to kiss him and bring back all those heated, glorious memories. Just this once, she told herself because she knew she and Reese had no future together. They'd hurt each other far too much to ever hope to heal past mistakes. And she'd never reveal him as her husband.

Never.

She lifted her mouth to his. The moment their lips touched, Reese took over, and she flowed farther into his arms, remembering how he'd always taken care with her.

He held her close and gently, but his kiss was harsh, pressing her lips roughly, and the mix of his musky scent and demanding body was the sweetest torture she'd ever known. He took from her and took some more, his lips crushing hers without tenderness or regard.

And just when she meant to push him away, realizing the punishing terms of his kiss, he softened his assault and the blending of their mouths turned into something she'd never expected to feel for Reese again—desire.

It burned through her.

She stood in his arms, stunned by her reaction.

She'd spent the last six years hating him for his betrayal, and in less than six minutes he'd made her want him again.

"Open for me, baby," he rasped out.

"Reese, this isn't—"

He mated their tongues, and her protest died quickly as old rhythms came back. The taste of him and the heady way he moved his mouth on hers sent shocking tingles down to her feet. She fell deeply into the kiss, unmindful of reason, throwing caution to the wind.

Don't fall for the guy again.

No, no. She wouldn't. She'd promised Nicole and herself. But she couldn't deny how alive he made her feel. More alive than she'd felt these past six years.

Reese broke off the kiss after long moments. "Still so pretty," he said, his breath caressing her lips. "Still taste so damn good."

Eliza's heart raced. A shocking thrill coursed down her body, making her tremble with need. His seductive tone had always promised a wild night tangling in the sheets.

"Touch me," he said quietly.

She lifted her hand to his face, her fingers outlining the strength of his jaw. She felt the contours, the slight stubble that shadowed his features, and remembered how that stubble would brush her thighs, creating rough friction against her legs right before he'd...

He bent his head and took her mouth again in another soul-searing kiss. Eliza kissed him back, caught up in memories she'd long ago buried. And when his knee parted her legs and he hiked her dress up slowly, the heat of his palm scorched her thigh. His fingers slid over her skin, inching higher until he teased the silken edge of her panties.

Wrapped in his embrace, devoured by his kiss, Eliza moaned deep in her throat. Her lower body pulsed in anticipation, waiting for a touch that would shatter her balanced world.

But Reese broke off the kiss, removed his hand from that highly sensitive area and lowered the hem of her dress. He took a step back, yet his smoldering gaze never left hers.

Disappointment registered, and she stood there, fully aroused, staring into unreadable eyes. No emotion flickered through, no regret or apology or frustration, none of the things Eliza felt right now, just that damnable blank stare. She watched him take a deep breath, grab his jacket and head for the door. "I have to go."

Eliza couldn't muster a response. She continued to watch him until finally he turned and smiled quickly, granting her a peek at one dimple that had always sent her heart humming. "Thanks for dinner."

She stood there, rooted to the spot until long after she heard Reese's car speed off.

"So is she off the hook?" Garrett asked as Reese rested his head against the bed pillow in his hotel room and clicked off the basketball game on television.

He spoke clearly into the phone. "Hell, no, she's not off the hook. She's very much *on* the hook."

"She found a woman in your bed. Most wives wouldn't look too kindly on that."

"Yeah, too bad I wasn't anywhere near that bed to reap the rewards."

Garrett paused for a long moment, then said, "Man, this really has thrown you, hasn't it?"

"Damn straight. She accused me of cheating on her, little brother. She should've known me better than that."

"Reese, you knew each other for all of—what?— three months. That's hardly enough time to—"

"To get married?"

"I didn't say that."

"It's what you and Pops thought. I know that. We got hitched exactly twenty-four days after we met. And less than ten weeks later the marriage was history."

"It doesn't matter what either of us thought at the time. What matters is what you're thinking now."

Reese lifted up from the bed, swung his legs out and braced his elbows on his knees, holding the phone tight against his ear. "I'm gonna finish this."

Garrett's frustrated sigh put Reese on edge. His brother had a history with women, but no woman had ever tied him down. He'd never allowed himself to get that close. Now Garrett was getting a taste of his own medicine with a woman who wouldn't look at him twice. Maybe Garrett was finally softening up to the idea of marriage. Whereas Reese had been there, done that—and it'd been a bitter pill to swallow.

"So how's Leanne?" he asked.

"Don't change the subject," Garrett snapped.

Reese smiled. Leanne was their top-notch geologist, a woman with brains and amazing good looks—and she didn't know that Garrett existed. At least that's the impression she'd always given. She'd been on their team from almost the beginning and had been invaluable to the company. Together, all three of them had made a fortune in the oil business. "Look, I know you have my best interests at heart, but don't worry about me. I know what I'm doing."

"That's exactly what worries me," Garrett said. "You can be…"

"Watch it, little bro."

"Tenacious. That's all I was going to say. You're damn tenacious when you go after something."

"Thanks. I'll take that as a compliment," Reese said, his sour mood lifting a bit.

"Tenacious *and* a giant pain in the ass."

Reese smiled.

"So you're coming home tomorrow?"

"Nice try. No, I'm staying in Sioux Falls for a little longer. As soon as I know my plans, I'll contact you."

"Don't forget you've got a company to run. And the damn decorator has left a dozen messages for you. Apparently she needs final approval before going ahead with the plans you've discussed. I'll thank you next time for not making me your middleman. I don't do plantation shutters versus pleated shades. Hell, half the time I don't know what that woman is talking about."

Reese grinned at Garrett's obvious frustration. He felt the same way. He'd wanted his house built to his specifications, but he didn't realize how much planning and thought went into furnishing and decorating it. He'd put that aspect of his new home on the back burner, but now he had some decisions to make about furnishing it to his liking. "I'll call her in the morning. You won't have to deal with her much longer. And, Garrett, thanks. I appreciate you holding down the fort while I'm away."

"You're welcome, but you're still a pain in the ass."

"One of my better qualities these days. Oh, and be sure to say hello to Leanne for me," he managed to get in before the connection died. He grinned when he heard a string of muttered curses from his brother on the other end.

Reese didn't know how he felt about Garrett falling for someone in the company. It could destroy their working relationship. But still, he wanted to see his brother happy, and if that meant him taking a chance, then so be it. Garrett, though, had yet to make his move.

Putting Garrett's love life out of his mind, he concentrated on his own, and the vision of a hot and passionate Eliza Fortune Parker slipped into his mind.

She'd hardly been off his mind lately.

She still reacted to him the same way she always had—with eager enthusiasm. Even though Reese knew she didn't want him anywhere near her or her precious family estate, her response to his advances told a different story. And Reese found he wanted to continue turning the pages to finish this book.

She was still his wife, damn it.

He'd have to do something about that soon.

Reese clicked on the television set again, lay down on the bed and tried to concentrate on a tied game with two teams racing down the clock, but he found himself staring blankly at the screen and thinking only of Eliza.

He'd once thought she'd left because he wasn't good enough for her, but he'd been mistaken. She hadn't run off just because of his lack of money. Hell, no. She saw him as a rodeo rider with no future, who had *cheated* on her.

He shoved aside the burning ache in his gut but held

on to his anger and whispered into the lonely hotel room, "Damn you, Eliza."

"I just don't know, Diana," Eliza said as she turned in a complete circle, taking yet another look at the cut glass, crystal and porcelain vases in the upscale boutique called Message on a Bottle. "I can't decide what's best for Gina and Case."

Diana—her friend, onetime college roommate and soon-to-be addition to the family as Max Fortune's wife—cast her a dubious look. "Hey, roomie, I've never known you to be indecisive. Especially when it comes to decorating. So what's up?"

Eliza stifled a groan. She'd asked Diana to tag along to help her pick out the centerpiece for Case and Gina's welcome-home celebration. Normally, Eliza needed no help when it came to setting a table, but she'd had trouble concentrating since Reese had shown up on her doorstep the other night. He'd overwhelmed her with his accusations, then stunned her even more with a kiss that had quickly escalated from simmering kindling to a raging fire within minutes.

A kiss that might have led to a wild tangling between the gossamer fabrics in her studio if Reese hadn't backed off. Lord, she'd barely been able think when his lips first touched hers. Her mind had taken flight and her traitorous body hadn't helped matters, either. She'd fallen into his touch, aching for his hands on her breasts, and then when he'd slid his hand up her thigh, she'd wanted him to go farther, the yearning in her deep and consuming. She'd wanted him to touch her until she splintered apart, one piece at a time.

Eliza shuddered at the notion.

She'd never thought she'd lay eyes on Reese again, much less have a heated confrontation with him. She'd spent the last two nights trying to justify what she'd seen in their hotel room six years ago. Reese's explanation had fully surprised her—he'd been merely helping a friend sober up. Nothing had happened.

After what she'd been through with Warren, she'd immediately jumped to conclusions seeing a woman in her bed. But had they been wrong conclusions? Her stomach was in knots. She hadn't eaten or slept much, thinking about Reese and whether or not she should have trusted him. Had he been innocent of any wrongdoing? Had she still been reeling from Warren's betrayal that she'd immediately seen the same in Reese without really thinking it through?

Still, finding a beautiful woman in her bed the minute she left town was pretty damning evidence, wasn't it? But if what Reese confessed was true, then Eliza had unwittingly thrown away the last six years of her life. *Their* life.

Her stomach squeezed tight, the pain searing through at the thought she might have destroyed everything because of her own insecurities. Still, Eliza clung to that one shred of doubt in her mind, that she might not have been wrong. What was fact and what was fiction? And did any of this really matter? She hadn't heard from Reese in two days. Maybe he'd already left town.

"Eliza," Diana said more forcefully, bringing Eliza's head up. "Are you okay today?"

"Oh…yes, I'm f-fine," she stuttered, trying to pull herself together. No sense alarming her friend. "I want this dinner to be perfect for Case and Gina."

Diana cast her a reassuring look. "It will be, Eliza. Everything you do is *perfect*."

If her friend only knew how imperfect her life really was, she'd be shocked. She had a secret husband, for one. A man who thought she'd left him because of his poor lifestyle—a man who may have been entirely innocent of her accusations of betrayal. A man she had loved with the whole of her heart yet couldn't reveal their relationship to anyone.

Having Diana here with her today helped direct her mind back to the dinner celebration tonight and off Reese Parker, his revelations and bold behavior the other night.

"I'm glad you were able to come along today," Eliza said. "You're good for my ego."

"It's the truth," Diana replied. "And I mean every word."

"Thank you," Eliza said, quite humbled, yet today she felt anything but perfect.

"It's great that we got a chance to become close again. If you hadn't suggested I come to live in Sioux Falls a few years ago, that might never have happened."

Eliza tossed aside her misgivings for the moment to smile at her friend. "As a bonus, you snagged yourself a gorgeous fiancé."

"There is that," she replied. "I would never have met up with Max again if it weren't for you."

"So now I'm a matchmaker?"

"You get some of the credit, yes."

Eliza was pleased how things had worked out for Diana and Max, though she knew she wouldn't have the same sort of happy ending in her life.

She glanced down at the twin overlapping hearts made of pewter that she held in her hand. Engraved with Case's and Gina's names and their wedding date, she'd have the proprietor set the plaque onto whatever vase they chose—the specialty of the boutique. A glorious array of fresh flowers would serve as the centerpiece for tonight's celebration as well as a welcome-home present for the two of them from the entire family.

But she couldn't seem to concentrate. Nothing struck her eye. Usually when on a mission like this, she knew exactly what she wanted and how to acquire it. Where had her professional acumen gone?

Never mind—she knew. But she couldn't divulge her secret to Diana. Though they'd been good friends and sorority sisters at Wellesley University, she would soon become a Fortune. Eliza wouldn't put a family member in the precarious position of keeping her secret.

She watched Diana stroll over to a display of tall, tapered, diamond-cut crystal vases. Diana ran her finger along one intricate vase, then peered up to meet her eyes.

Putting Reese completely out of her mind, Eliza walked over to the display table. "I think you've found it." She lifted the vase and examined it carefully. "We'll take this one," she said to Diana. "It'll be…"

"*Perfect*," they chorused.

Nash Fortune smiled with warmth at his son and new daughter-in-law, raising his champagne glass in a toast.

"Let's welcome home the newlyweds in true Fortune style," he said as the family circled the couple in the great room and lifted their glasses. "May Case and Gina always know happiness and love." Then Eliza's father cast a loving glance at his wife, Patricia. "My wish for you both is a loving relationship filled with honesty and trust."

Patricia's smile was tentative, her lips trembling, her eyes blinking away tears. Nash took his wife's hand, and for a moment Eliza noted distress in his eyes right before he grinned. "And maybe a grandchild or two."

"We'll get right on that, Dad," Case said and everyone laughed. Everyone but Patricia. She seemed a million miles away.

"You do that, son."

Then the room ignited with conversation. When the Fortune family got together, it wasn't a quiet affair. Glasses clinked, voices mingled and laughter filled the room. Family gatherings weren't always so joyous, though. Most times it was a meeting of minds behind the Fortune empire and a way to connect the business dots camouflaged as a family function. But today was all about Case and his new wife. Eliza found herself relaxing with the newlyweds and Diana and Max, her brother, Creed, her half sister, Skylar, and her parents. Maya was on her way to the celebration and Blake had refused the invitation. A good thing, too, because Blake held no fondness for either Case or Creed, the half brothers always butting heads.

So for the first time since Reese had shown up at the charity auction, Eliza could let down her guard.

Twenty minutes later, the family sat down for their

meal in the dining room. Ivy had outdone herself with a sumptuous display of seafood—oysters, crab cakes, baked halibut and lobster tails drenched in drawn butter. Vegetables and side dishes complemented the meal, as well as four different kinds of breads and muffins. Eliza's floral arrangement centered the oblong table, standing tall enough to allow everyone's eyes to meet without obstruction.

"Oh, the flowers and vase are lovely," Gina said instantly, noting the inscription. "This has to be your doing, Eliza."

"Yeah, thanks, sis," Case said, glancing at their names and wedding date engraved on the vase. "At least this way I'll never forget our anniversary."

Gina smiled at Case and in a teasing tone said, "Yes, it'll help jog my memory, too."

Case grabbed hold of Gina's hand, bringing it to his lips for a quick kiss. "I have other ways to jog your memory, sweetheart."

Nash smiled and turned to Patricia. "Maybe we're not too far off from those grandkids."

"What? Oh…yes. Grandkids. That would be…nice." Patricia forced a smile.

"I'm happy you like it," Eliza said, "but I can't take full credit. Diana actually picked it out. She did a wonderful job."

Eliza spoke to Case and Gina, but it was Patricia's distracted behavior tonight that held her attention. Eliza knew something about keeping up a pretense and wondered if Patricia was upset or hiding something terribly important. She'd never seen her so…troubled.

And a minute later the doorbell chimed. "I bet that's Maya. I'll let her in," her father said, rising to answer the door.

If anyone could shake Patricia out of her doldrums, it would be her only daughter, Maya. It seemed that Eliza's father was anxious to please his wife, something he'd done ever since they'd first married thirteen years ago.

When Nash returned to the dining room, all eyes lifted. "Well, it wasn't Maya at the door, but we do have another guest. Eliza, this young man came to see you tonight, and I invited him to join us for dinner. Why don't you introduce him to the family?"

Startled, Eliza's gaze darted from her father to the tall, good-looking man standing beside him wearing Armani and an easy smile.

Reese.

Her heart slammed against her chest and her mind raced with questions. Why was he here? Had he given away their secret? Was he planning to? A piece of bread she'd been chewing stuck in her throat. She forced herself to swallow it down. Trapped amid a family showing more than slight interest, Eliza had no choice but to make the introductions.

Slowly, with feigned composure, she took a breath and rose on shaky legs to look him straight in the eye. She prayed that he wouldn't ruin the evening. "Everyone, I'd like you to meet Reese…Parkman."

"Parker," Reese corrected, his dark eyes narrowing on her.

"Eliza, why don't you show Mr. Parker to his seat," her father said.

Eliza hesitated, darting a glance around the room to all the family members she'd lied to over the years. Oh, God. This couldn't be happening.

"If it wouldn't be too much trouble, ma'am," Reese said casually.

Sinking fast with no one to throw her a rope, Eliza managed to say, "Of course...no trouble at all."

As if Reese Parker, her secret husband, the man who could turn her world upside down, didn't know how much his appearance here tonight would cause her nothing *but* trouble.

Four

"You say you're from Montana?" Nash asked Reese after all the introductions and handshakes were made. Reese settled back in his seat, with Creed Fortune to his right and Max Fortune to his left, Eliza seating him on the opposite side of the table from her. But from his vantage point, he could look directly into her eyes. Eyes that so far refused to meet his.

"Yes, sir. Born and raised." He sipped wine.

"The oil business must be pretty good these days," Nash said matter-of-factly. "You made a hefty contribution to Eliza's fund-raiser the other night, which was very kind."

Reese shrugged. "I have a soft spot for keeping the Old West alive. It was my way of helping the museum."

Nash glanced at Eliza, and when she didn't respond,

he continued, "My daddy, Charles Fortune, made the bulk of his wealth as a wildcatter back in 1929. It's a tough business. A man's got to have a lot of stamina to stick it out."

"And some financial support," Creed added.

Reese agreed. "That's true. I didn't have much of the latter, but I guess I'm stubborn enough when I want something. I worked my way through the rodeo circuit as a bareback bronc rider, winning some competitions and scraping by. I poured everything I had into wildcatting. The standing joke was that I couldn't find oil in a gas station."

Nash Fortune eyed him carefully. "But you proved them wrong."

Reese nodded, then glanced at Eliza, who had suddenly lifted her eyes to meet his. "You could say that I proved myself *right*."

The men at the table nodded in understanding.

Eliza shuffled in her seat and looked away, the food on her plate untouched. Clearly, she didn't want him here. Reese could take satisfaction in that, watching color rise in her cheeks and her chest heave with quiet indignation. She wore sparkling blue sapphires in her ears and around her neck, bringing out the deep blue in her eyes. Her blond hair was twisted up into some sort of elegant knot, with those long bangs softly caressing her brows. She'd dressed modestly tonight; the conservative silk blouse unbuttoned at the throat left the rest up to the imagination. And Reese did imagine undoing each one of the those buttons until he could slip his hands inside and...

"Didn't you spend a summer in Montana, Eliza?" Creed asked innocently, his gaze fixed on his sister.

She froze for a moment and those pretty blue eyes widened with a fear only Reese might have noticed. She sipped wine before answering. "Yes…I did. One summer." She cleared her throat delicately, then added, "I didn't stay in one place long, though. I, uh, did some traveling from place to place."

"It's big-sky country. People don't usually bump into each other unless it's intentional," Reese stated. Then, setting his gaze on Eliza, he added, "But trust me, if I met Eliza in Montana, *I wouldn't have forgotten.*"

Eliza shifted her focus to him, her expression bordering on dread.

Silence ensued as Nash raised an eyebrow at his daughter. The other family members stared at her, too—with more interest than she'd like, he guessed—before fixing their stares back on him. But Reese only watched Eliza. And he didn't find the wildly erotic, carefree woman he'd married that summer seated across from him. Instead she seemed subdued, unsure and, most of all, inhibited. Not at all the same woman he'd known.

Case broke the silence. "Well, Eliza might not have met you before, but you sure as hell look familiar to me. Though, I can't recall ever meeting you."

Reese stifled a sharp response. Hell, yes, they'd met. The day he'd come here to retrieve his wife, six years ago. He'd been tossed off the property by an overprotective brother who'd wanted "no damn drunken cowboy" lurking on his property. Hell, the man had offered to have him thrown in jail. Reese hadn't divulged any information. He hadn't told Case he had a perfect right to be there since he was married to his sister. No, Reese hadn't given away Eliza's wretched secret. Instead he'd gotten the Fortune message, loud and clear.

Reese smiled. "I guess I have that kind of face."

Even from across the table, he noticed Eliza exhaling her breath slowly in somewhat relief.

"So what brings you to Sioux Falls?" Nash asked, but Reese got the distinct impression the man wanted to know what he was doing knocking on his door, looking for Eliza.

"I'm here on business." Personal business, he didn't add. "Looking to acquire some horses for the stables I plan to build on my property just outside of Bozeman. I've got an eight-thousand-square-foot home sitting on a hundred and fifty acres of land. When Eliza cooked me dinner the other night, she mentioned that she knew something about interior design. I thought maybe she could help me out a little."

Eliza's expression turned from barely contained surprise to out-and-out astonishment.

"Eliza's done nice work on this home, but—" Nash began, until his wife laid a hand on his arm, halting his next thought.

"Eliza is very talented," Patricia said quietly, speaking up for the first time since Reese had met her. "She has an eye for color and design. As a teenager, she was always rearranging things and making them look better."

Eliza peered at her stepmother with gratitude in her eyes.

Gina added, "I've already requested that she do up the baby nursery when the time comes."

All heads turned her way. "I said *when* the time comes. No need to get excited. I'm not keeping any secrets."

Creed Fortune twisted his mouth, his tone dry. "Heaven forbid a Fortune keeps a secret."

Patricia's face paled almost as much as Eliza's. The rest of the Fortunes kept their mouths clamped shut with that remark, and Reese wondered what other secrets were contained in this room.

But when a pretty, dark-haired young woman walked into the dining room, all attention turned to her.

"Hello, everyone. Sorry I missed dinner." She walked over to give Patricia a kiss on the cheek. "Hi, Mom."

She was greeted with pleasantries from everyone but Creed. Reese had heard his sharp intake of breath when she'd walked in.

"Maya? Oh, hello, dear." Patricia took her daughter's hand.

Nash rose immediately. "Sit with your mother, Maya. I'll just get another—"

"No, there's no need. I'm not staying long. I just dropped by to say hello and welcome Gina and Case home from their honeymoon."

"You're not staying?" Nash asked, unable to mask his disappointment. "Your mother's been looking forward to seeing you. We all have."

Maya blinked, then doubt crept into her eyes. "I can't this time."

"Well, before you go, let me introduce you to our guest. Reese Parker, this is Patricia's daughter, Maya. Maya, Reese."

Reese rose and acknowledged her. "Nice to meet you."

Maya responded politely, but her gaze drifted over to Creed and the two exchanged glances.

"Maya, how's Brad these days? We haven't seen him in a while," Eliza asked.

"He's fine. Brad's out of town until tomorrow night. He's—"

"He's never around unless he wants something," Creed said curtly.

"That's not true!" Maya's dark brown eyes burned with denial.

Creed almost came out of his chair. "He's using you, Maya. When will you open your eyes? He wants to put his hands on Fortune money. He's already put his hands on yo—"

"Creed!" Eliza's voice rose to an uneven pitch. "Stop right there."

Maya's face flamed and tears filled her eyes. "Shut up, Creed. You don't know what you're talking about."

"Settle down. Both of you," Nash said in the same way he might have scolded them when they were children, the father overseeing his son and stepdaughter. "Creed, you're out of line."

Patricia rose from her seat and spoke directly to Creed. "You've upset Maya."

"She needs upsetting, Patricia. She needs to see what that boyfriend of hers—"

"Enough!" Maya said, stomping her foot. Then her

voice wobbled when she said, "I won't h-hear a-another word. Sorry, Mom…but I…can't stay." She burst into tears and ran from the room.

Eliza tossed her napkin down and glared at her brother. "That was productive." She rose from the table and spoke to Patricia in a soothing soft voice. "I'll go talk to her."

"Talk some sense into her, will you?" Creed remarked.

Patricia frowned at Creed, then looked at her husband. "I'm going upstairs. This is all too much for me." She glanced at Reese, then the others. "I'm terribly sorry. Please excuse me."

Nash blinked and then flung his napkin down, waiting until his wife was out of the room before confronting his son. "What's gotten into you, Creed?"

Reese rose then, ready to make his escape. "This is a family matter and I'm intruding. Please tell Eliza I'll wait for her outside. Thank you for dinner."

Nash apologized and walked him to the front door.

Once outside, Reese grabbed hold of fresh South Dakota air thanking God he wasn't born into a large family.

Eliza wrapped her arms around her middle and walked outside, ready to head off another disaster. She'd spoken with Maya and had managed to calm her down a little. She'd encouraged her younger stepsister to go upstairs and spend some time with her mother. Eliza didn't know what was going on with Patricia, but Maya had always been able to put joy in her mother's eyes. They both needed each other tonight.

And Eliza wondered, if she'd had her own mother right now, would she be able to comfort her, as well? What Eliza needed right now was a warm heart, a good ear and caring arms surrounding her with unconditional love—a mother's love. Sadly Eliza would never know that kind of love.

She found Reese waiting for her. He stood leaning up against his car, that long, lean, incredibly fit body turned away from her, his jacket tossed aside. She walked around the car to face him from a distance as moonlight shadowed his features. "Well, that's my family."

Reese looked into her eyes. "Man, is it always like that?"

Eliza shrugged. She didn't owe Reese an explanation, yet she wanted to give him one anyway. "No, not always. But there are a lot of personalities to deal with. Ego, pride and mulishness add to the mix. But there's love, too. Sometimes it gets hidden between all the turmoil, but it's tucked in there and we all know it."

Reese nodded, but she doubted he really understood.

When she shivered from the March breezes blowing by, Reese approached her and laid his jacket over her shoulders.

She hugged the lapels, closing the jacket to keep her warm as the scent of pine and Reese enveloped her. She'd always loved the scent of him, his raw, earthy power and the maleness that defined him. "What are you doing here?"

"Besides having dinner with my...wife?"

"Shhh. Keep your voice down."

"No one can hear me out here, Eliza. If you weren't so bent on keeping your marital status a secret, you wouldn't walk around worrying yourself to death that you might disappoint someone in the family. Clearly they are too wrapped up in themselves to care about your one digression."

That's not true, she wanted to say. But what good would arguing the point do? She couldn't reveal Reese as her husband and didn't know if she'd even want to. "Why did you show up here?" she asked again.

Reese jammed his hands in his trousers and leaned back against his car. He stared up into a cool, cloudless night sky. She watched his throat work as he formulated the words. "My father died last month."

"Oh! I'm so sorry. He was…kind to me and a nice man."

"He liked you," he said in a rare unguarded moment. His smile was quick, revealing that one sexy dimple that set her equilibrium on tilt. "I promised him I'd get my life in order."

"How do you plan on doing that?" she asked, still reeling from the news of his father's death.

"There's only one way," he said, then turned the full force of his focus on her. His eyes probed hers for a moment, his look resolute. "Divorce. I have the papers in my hotel room."

Eliza blinked and stifled the surprised "oh" she wanted to exclaim. Of course she knew eventually something had to be done regarding their marriage, but she'd put off the inevitable in her mind until the thought had become fleeting and distant. But now she had to deal in reality. Reese was here. And he wanted a divorce. "Okay."

"Okay?" A fierce emotion passed over Reese's expression before he nodded. "Can you get away tonight?"

He was eager to be rid of her. Eliza wondered if there was a woman or two in his life, and the thought troubled her much more than it should. "The evening's ruined. I won't be missed."

Ironically, Reese had taken pleasure in giving her family reason to believe he was interested in her, when in fact, the true motive for his arrival tonight was to liberate himself from her entirely. "Just give me a minute to grab my purse and jacket."

"Take your time," he said to her back as she headed toward the house. "I've waited six years…I can wait a few more minutes."

She stood with her back against his penthouse door, jittery as a schoolgirl with her first crush. The pop of a champagne cork made her jump as she watched Reese behind the bar working a bottle, pouring overflowing bubbles into two tall flutes. "Champagne?"

Reese's face held no emotion. "I couldn't afford to begin our marriage this way."

"So we'll toast the end of our marriage, is that it?"

"Something like that." He motioned for her to come farther into the room. "I don't bite, darlin'."

"That's not how I remember it," she blurted, then a warmth flamed her face. Eliza rarely blushed, but the memory of Reese—that mouth, those teeth—flashed quickly in her mind.

Reese's head shot up and their eyes met. He smiled, a genuine, full-out sexy-as-sin smile with that dimple peeking out, and Eliza's whole body went hot.

"Yeah, I guess you're right." He walked over to her and handed her a glass. "To getting our lives back." He sipped from his glass, then strode to the window to stare out at the Sioux Falls skyline.

Eliza stepped farther into the large, elegant room, making note of the decor almost unconsciously, while fully aware of Reese and the new kind of power he held. Money could do that—it could change a man. And Reese seemed different in so many ways. She would never have pictured him in a luxurious penthouse suite, for one, with money to burn and a lifestyle he might have only dreamed about. But he'd done it. He'd made a success of his life despite the hardships and the heartaches he'd endured. That's if what he'd told her was true. If he had been faithful to her during that brief time in their life.

"Since this may be," she began, chewing on her lower lip, "the last time we see each other, please let me say that I'm happy for you, Reese. You accomplished what you set out to accomplish."

Reese whipped around from the window. "Did I?"

Eliza blinked and cast him a curious look. "Didn't you?"

He stared at her for a long moment, a tick in his jaw pacing out a slow beat. "Success in my professional life, failure in my personal life. I think that's fifty-fifty."

"You're not a failure."

He snorted before gulping down his drink. "Darlin', we both failed, didn't we?"

Her champagne went down just as harsh as his words. It'd been a trying night, and now as she faced Reese on rubbery legs, she hated to admit the truth. "I suppose." She sat down on the chintz sofa and leaned back against a pretty pillow before her legs could give way. "Do you think we can keep this—I mean…the divorce—quiet?"

"Sure. Why not?" he said gruffly.

Eliza winced inwardly. "It's just that—"

"Damn it, don't bother explaining again. I get it. I always have. Since we married in Montana, it shouldn't be a problem. No one here has to know."

With shaky hands, Eliza set her glass down on the marble coffee table then clumsily knocked it over onto some papers that were sprawled out. "Oh, I'm so sorry." The champagne washed away some of the print. "These aren't the—"

"No," he answered, bringing over a bar towel to blot the papers dry. "Don't worry about it." He grabbed up the papers and looked them over. "I have another copy."

"What are they?" she asked curiously.

"The layout of my house," he said absently. "The designer is giving my brother a hard time back home. She needs to get started on a few rooms, and I can't make up my mind."

"Oh, yes," Eliza said, recalling the lie Reese told the family about his visit to her tonight. "The house you'd wanted me to help you with."

Reese looked over the top of the papers to stare at her. "I had to think fast on my feet."

Eliza smiled. "You were sitting down so that would make you fast on your…"

Reese lifted a brow. "God, I thought you'd lost your sense of humor."

"I haven't had much to laugh about lately." Eliza let go of her smile. She didn't realize it until just now, but there was more truth in her words than she'd like to acknowledge.

He frowned at that, then sat down right next to her, so close that the musky pine scent of him stirred her senses. "Since you're here, do you want to take a look?"

"I'd never pass up a chance," she said as she slid the papers from his hands to hers, "to take a look at designs." She studied the papers, room upon room, and the designer's ideas that were marked on the layouts. When she was through, she shook her head. She knew Reese. Well, she'd known Reese Parker, and what the designer had in mind was completely wrong.

"What?" he said, genuinely interested.

"Does the designer know you, at all?"

"No, but she came highly recommended."

"And did you discuss what you wanted for the house?"

Reese nodded. "Yeah, but not in any great detail. That's her job, isn't it?"

Eliza took a deep breath. "A good designer has to know the person she's dealing with. She has to get a feel for what you want. I doubt you want white marble for a fireplace, Reese. Or alabaster walls or a wet bar made of beveled glass." Then doubt crept in and Eliza wondered if Reese had changed more than she'd thought. Maybe he did want a modern house with trendy designs. "Or maybe you do?"

"I don't," he said emphatically. His face was just inches from hers, and when he turned, the force of his gaze on her, those dark brown eyes held her transfixed. "Tell me what you'd do," he said softly.

Eliza hesitated for a long moment. Could she afford to give him her ideas, to expose herself so openly and feel the undeniable temptation of work she craved, while trying to ignore the forbidden temptation Reese posed to her? He was the husband she couldn't claim, after all. Shouldn't she just fold up the layouts and leave?

She should.

But the work—it was far too strong an enticement.

So for the next thirty minutes she sat with Reese and they discussed his ideas and hers. They drank champagne to the last drop and, with heads together, became fully immersed in designing Reese's new home.

Once they'd discussed every room and there was nothing more to say, Eliza rose, feeling tipsy and too excited for her own good. She and Reese had come up with some great ideas together, but she wouldn't deceive herself—she'd never see her designs come to fruition.

"You'd better take me home now," she said. She grabbed her purse and jacket, then turned toward the door.

"Eliza, come back here," Reese commanded gently.

She swiveled around to find him standing by the sofa, his shirtsleeves rolled up to his elbows, his tie gone, his dark eyes gleaming and his tone reminiscent of the man she'd once loved. He looked sexy and dangerous, and before she could stop herself, she moved closer to him. "That's right, we forgot about the divorce pap—"

His lips came down on hers hard, obliterating her last words, and as he pulled her into his embrace, he also obliterated all rational thoughts she might have had. The kiss went long and deep, champagne mingling with warm lips and hot bodies and the feel of Reese's erection pressing on her ignited a fire inside her.

And when their lips finally broke apart the question must have still been in her eyes, because Reese quickly responded, "There's time for that, darlin'."

He took her hand then and, as he lowered himself down on the sofa, one tug had her falling into his lap. He pulled the knot of her hair loose, and pins went flying right before his lips met hers again. He held her close with one hand, while the other played with the strands of her hair, lacing his fingers through until he cupped her head and dipped her low. She fell back against the sofa cushion, and he followed her down, kissing her again, his lips and tongue taking pleasure and giving it fully in return.

He slid his hand down to her blouse, and buttons flew open. She felt the cool air caress her skin before hot fingers skimmed over the lace of her bra. Underneath, her nipples hardened, awaiting his touch, and when he finally pushed aside the material, he didn't disappoint. His fingers teased and tempted and he whispered in her ear what he wanted from her. The commands, the way he spoke to her, the way he touched her sent every nerve ending tingling.

"I have to be inside you," he whispered urgently.

Yes, she wanted that, too. So much. "We can't," she said, surprising herself.

"We are, baby."

"It's been six years, Reese," she breathed out.

"Making up for lost time." He nibbled on her throat.

Eliza ached from the pleasure, from having Reese want her, from feeling desirable again. She pushed his chest just hard enough for him to lift up and look deeply into her eyes. "There hasn't been anyone…else. Not in six years." She slid her eyes closed for a moment, then faced him again. "Can you say the same?"

Reese stared at her, his dark eyes burning like black coals. He shook his head briskly. "You have no right asking me that, Eliza. Not when you walked out on me without looking back."

Reese untangled his body from hers. He sat up on the sofa and slammed his body back against the cushion. Eliza rose from her prone position to sit next to him. With trembling fingers, she buttoned her blouse and tried to finger-comb her unruly hair.

"Is there someone else?" she asked quietly, setting her pride aside.

Reese remained silent.

Searing pain worked its way into her stomach, though she fought it tooth and nail. She'd put the past behind her, and now that Reese had returned, he'd managed to wedge his way in, causing her more anxiety and hurt.

She stood and grabbed hold of her jacket and purse, then headed to the door. She should have walked out before. If she had, the grim reality that she may have pushed a loving husband into another woman's arms might not be haunting her thoughts. But it was there, along with the rest of the confusion Reese Parker's appearance had brought about. And there wasn't much she could do about any of it.

Not after the pain they'd caused each other.

Not after the lies she'd told.

Not after winning the battle to give up on Reese years ago.

"I'll take a taxi home."

But before she reached the door, he was there, jamming his arms into his jacket and opening the door for her. "I'll drive you."

Five

Reese slowed the car to a stop before reaching the gates of the Fortune estate. He put the car in Park, set one arm on the steering wheel and turned to look at Eliza. She'd been quiet on the ride home. No sense making small talk. They'd both been too wrapped up in their own thoughts. In the four hours he'd spent with her tonight, he'd known a wealth of emotions, the last being fury at his estranged wife. Had she truly expected him to answer her question? Had she wanted to hear the truth? Had she expected him to live the life of a monk after she'd walked out on him?

He still wanted her; he couldn't deny it. But he'd never get over her mistrust in him. He'd been looking forward to a future with her, having babies, growing old. But she'd thrown it all away. And, damn it, before she signed those legal papers terminating their sorry marriage, Reese had to be through with her in his mind, his heart and his body.

Then he'd truly be free.

"Things got a little crazy back there," he said.

Eliza put her head down. "It always did when we got together, but I thought after six years that might have changed."

"Guess we found out it didn't."

When she nodded, her blond hair fell onto her face, and Reese reached over to gently brush it away. She looked up at him with a tentative smile. "I'll sign the divorce papers whenever you want. Did you bring them with you?"

Reese lifted his arms in a gesture of futility. "It wasn't the first thing on my mind."

She lifted her chin, and he noted the pretty blue sparkle in her eyes and her hair in wild disarray around her face. "What was?"

"Stripping you naked. Getting laid. Having incredible sex. Take your pick, darlin'."

She gasped, and her sharp intake of breath echoed through the silence. "We can't go back, Reese."

"Don't want to."

"Then what *do* you want from me?"

"I guess I didn't know until tonight." He scratched his head and went for broke. "I want you to come to Montana with me."

"What? I can't do th—"

"It's a business proposition. I want you to take a look at my house. I want you to see it firsthand and tell

me how to make it a home. You must have said it yourself a dozen times tonight—that you wished you could
see the place in person."

"Yes, but I didn't mean it literally."

"You have good ideas. You know me better than anyone else I might hire. I'm not asking you to do the work."

No, he didn't want to commit himself to hiring her
on as his designer, but he wanted her to see his house.
Not only for her design ideas but because with every
dollar he made, every oil rig that blew, every time he'd
proven himself a success, he thought of her. And now he
wanted her to see the full extent of what she'd thrown
away.

"Just come and take a look. I can have a plane waiting at sunup and you'll be home before sundown. This
house means a lot to me, Eliza. I don't want to make
any mistakes."

"It would be very…awkward, Reese. If you have
a—"

"Damn it, Eliza. I'm not building this house for anyone but me. There's a cottage on the property that's
finished. My father and I lived there together for a short
time. The place was going to be his. But now he's gone.
I'm not asking you to design something for another
woman. Hell, I don't know a woman who would stand
for that, do you?"

"No…no. But I don't know…" Yet as she spoke
the words, a light flickered in her eyes. Through the
hazy moonlight shining inside the Jaguar, Reese
could see that he'd sparked her interest. No one at the
Fortune house seemed to take her work seriously. It

hadn't taken him long to figure that out. Now, he offered her something she'd always wanted, and she'd be foolish to turn him down.

"I'm asking for just one day. C'mon, Eliza. Where's that free-spirited woman I met six years ago? Don't think too hard, just do it."

Eliza stared out the window for a long time. Reese was about to argue another round with her, but she turned suddenly with determination written on her face. "What time tomorrow?"

"I'll pick you up at seven."

"I'll be ready."

"Fine."

Satisfied, Reese started the engine, but Eliza put a hand out. "Don't drive me inside the gates. I want to walk. I need to clear my head."

Reese slid out of the car and opened the door for her. After she wished him a good night, Reese watched her walk away.

Tomorrow, he planned on making her clear head dizzy again.

"You're up early, Eliza," her father said, sipping coffee by the breakfast table. He eyed her up and down, making mental notes of her appearance.

She wore comfortable clothes today—jeans, a black V-neck sweater and a pair of boots, usual apparel for some women, but not for Eliza. Not since she'd spent the summer following Reese around the rodeo, getting her hands dirty on corral fences, trailer hitches and barbecue grills. And her father had noticed. Though he'd retired to spend more time with Patricia, his mind was as sharp as a tack and he hardly missed a thing.

Except, of course, the secret marriage she'd kept from the entire family. She could be deceptive when necessary and she'd hated every minute of fooling him and everyone else she'd cared about. The whole darn situation had escalated without conscious thought, and now, six years later, it was too late to untwist the lies.

"I have an appointment. Don't worry if I'm not home until late tonight." Eliza poured herself a cup of French roast, grabbed a croissant and swiveled around to make a quick exit. No sense adding to the deception.

"What kind of appointment?"

Trapped, Eliza decided not to lie. The truth wouldn't hurt in this case. She turned with the coffee cup to her lips, adding casually. "Just a design project. I'm going to take a look at someone's house and—"

"Dressed like that?" He shook his head. "You're off to Montana. It's Parker's house, isn't it?"

Sharp as a tack.

Okay, she thought, at least Reese had given her a way out of this. "Yes, no big surprise. He'd mentioned it yesterday at dinner."

"He's flying you there?"

She nodded. "Private jet."

Her father opened the *Tribune* and nodded. "It's about time you had a man in your life."

"Dad!" She nearly spilled coffee onto the floor. What could she say without telling more lies? At the moment, Reese was the man in her life, but not in the way her father assumed. "I'm hardly eighteen, going out on a date. It's business."

He lowered the newspaper and peered over at her. "I won't worry if you don't make it home tonight."

"Oh, I'll be here. It's just a day trip."

"If you say so. You're a big girl," he said as she walked over to him to plant a quick guilt-ridden kiss on his cheek, praying the lies would end soon.

"See you *tonight,* Dad," she made a point of saying.

Reese was prompt picking her up. She met him outside and didn't wait for him to get out of the car to open her door. She grabbed the handle and watched him slide his body over to open the door from the inside. With a push, it opened and Eliza took her seat. The fresh scent of shampoo and soap and pine struck her instantly, the heady mix permeating the interior of the car. Eliza tried to ignore how that scent affected her, but she couldn't quite disregard the way Reese looked this morning.

In beat-up boots, faded jeans and a tan chambray shirt, he hardly appeared the smooth oil executive with his own private jet, but rather he reminded her of the ruggedly sexy cowboy she'd met at a rodeo one sizzling hot summer day. His big silver belt buckle set across a trim rippled abdomen—a trophy of a championship win—caught the early morning light and her full attention. "Good morning," she said stiffly, wanting to keep a professional distance.

Reese's gaze traveled over her suede jacket to the *V* of her neckline, lingering there for a moment before he lifted his eyes to hers. She silently cursed her vivid memory—a flash of his hands and mouth on her skin and the way she'd come alive from his touch last night.

"You came prepared."

She glanced at the briefcase she held on her lap. "Just some samples, colors, ideas I jotted down."

He took off and they drove toward the airport, the radio filling the silence, a sweet country ballad that lulled her nerves.

"I like the look," he said, keeping his eyes on the road. And Eliza felt as though they'd gone back in time, when they'd dressed this way every single day.

When they reached the airport, Reese guided her onto the Gulfstream 200, and she took a seat on a cream-colored leather chair. "Get settled in," he said. "I'll check with the pilot. We should be taking off soon."

Reese disappeared into the cockpit and Eliza released her breath. What was she doing? Going back to Montana would only stir up old feelings. Feelings she'd put to rest long ago. Yet she had to admit she was curious about Reese, his home and his life. The final temptation came with seeing the layout of his very unique home. There was so much potential—empty walls and uncovered windows that needed just the right touch to make the house a home.

When Reese returned with a smile on his face, chuckling from something the pilot said, Eliza might have melted in a puddle. She remembered that hearty laugh, the richness in his dark eyes when something amused him and that darn dimple peeking out.

"Buckle up," he said, the smile still on his face. "We'll be taking off in two minutes."

"Okay," she said.

Reese sat across from her, latching his belt. Once they were in the air, he said, "I've got some reports to go over." He pointed to the window. "Enjoy the view. We'll be in Montana before you know it."

He got up to sit behind a table that also served as his desk, and Eliza did enjoy the view, both the one below her and one the sitting a few feet away, deep in concentration.

Today he seemed all business, whereas last night he'd hardly been in a business-minded mood at all. She couldn't quite figure him out. He'd seemed so intent on divorcing her, but now she didn't know what to think.

So much had changed in the last six years, but when she'd been in his arms last night, it seemed as if nothing had changed at all.

They arrived at Gallatin Field in Bozeman before nine. Reese ushered her off the plane and into his car, this time not an elegant Jag but a Yukon, with all the bells, whistles and buttons one could imagine. "Button up—there's a chill in the air."

Reese reached into the backseat, coming up with a tan Stetson hat. He plunked it onto her head, and even though he tried, he couldn't conceal a grin. "Bet you haven't worn one of these for a while."

Eliza laughed. "Not true," she said as they began the drive. "I headed a fund-raiser for a children's hospital once. We all dressed up like this and had lasso lessons, sang country songs, square-danced."

"Where, inside a ballroom?" he asked in a mocking tone.

"No, not inside a ballroom," she bantered back. "At Burt Candlewood's ranch. He'd lost his son to a rare disease," she said, unable to hide the emotion in her voice. The memory of that family's grief struck Eliza anew. She'd always wanted children. Adored them, really. She couldn't imagine the pain of losing your own child. "We raised a good deal of money that day."

Reese took his eyes off the road for a moment, his gaze studying her, before he nodded and turned his attention onto the highway again.

Eliza wrapped her arms around her middle, the descending cold temperature sending a chill through her body as they drove on.

"I've got warmer clothes at the cottage," Reese said.

"I should have known better. The weather can change quickly this time of year."

Twenty minutes later, Reese pulled to a stop on a hilly rise. From there, Eliza followed the direction of his gaze. Twin columns of stately blue spruce trees edged the road leading to the main house. The house, though, stole all of her breath, with its trilevel splendor. New England cottage stone framed the large paned windows. Timber beams braced the second story with a mix of stone and cedar shakes. As Reese drove forward onto a pebbled circular driveway, Eliza gasped in awe when the entry of the house came into view. "Oh…wow."

Oh, wow? That's all she could manage to say about a house that she would die to focus her talent on? Strategetically placed flagstone steps led to a split entryway where doors to the left and right allowed entrance to the house. The second story sat above a hollowed-out area below known as an outdoor living room, complete with a rock fireplace. Eliza had only seen this done once before. Already she envisioned filling that space with an array of sturdy outdoor furniture.

"Come on, I'll give you the nickel tour," he said, and Eliza bounded out of the SUV.

"I've never seen such an architectural design done like this for a single-family dwelling. This is amazing, Reese," she said as he came around the SUV, but Eliza had already taken off toward the outdoor living room. She whirled around, taking it all in.

"This sold me on the house. This *and* the view." Reese pointed through the living space to a spot beyond, and Eliza strode over to where the living space converged onto a log-railed terrace. From that point, a small lake came into view, the clouded morning sun shedding a stingy amount of light onto the water. Eliza could only imagine the lake, surrounded by tall pines and mountains, when the sun cast its full wrath of light onto the waters.

Her heart thudded in her chest. The view was breathtaking. "I saw the layouts, but nothing compares to seeing it in person."

"Want to see the inside?" Reese asked.

Eliza tore her gaze away from the stunning view and nodded, following Reese inside the house.

"There's seventeen rooms," he said as they went inside.

Eliza let her gaze flow around the three rooms she

could see from her vantage point—the great room that faced the back view of the lake and surroundings, an area for dining, also facing the lake, and beyond that the eating area of the kitchen. All open, all wide, glorious windows, all spectacular spaces that held amazing promise if done correctly.

She glanced first at the unfinished fireplace and hearth. "I see stacked slate here, all the way to the high beamed ceiling. A solid carved mantel…dark pine. And bookcases on both sides. Wood flooring in this room, maybe throughout the entire first floor. What other rooms are on this floor?"

"There's a wine cellar just off the kitchen, a more formal living room and the master bedroom."

"And upstairs?" she said, looking at the staircase that separated the living space from the eating areas.

"Well…" Reese said with a look of deep concentration. "There's a recreation room, a gym, home office and steps up from there, two attic bedrooms—what they call sky bedrooms—and a sitting room that overlooks the lake and joins the wings of the house."

Eliza had been pretty good at reading home plans and layouts and she'd gotten a feel about this house from what she'd seen in Reese's hotel room last night, but being here and seeing the potential this house had boggled her mind.

She itched to get her hands on it.

The challenge would be tremendous and one she'd love to take on…and if it were anyone else's home, she'd be secretly dreaming up ways to get the commission.

But this was her soon-to-be ex-husband's house. The

complications were too numerous to even consider. Besides which, Reese hadn't asked her. He'd only wanted her opinion.

And that also baffled her.

Why would he *want* her opinion about anything when he'd been so incredibly angry with her?

"Let's go up," she said.

"After you." Reese gestured for her to take the stairs.

And twenty minutes later Eliza had mentally filled the entire second floor with furniture, artwork and window treatments. She took the short steps up to the third level to view two attic bedrooms with slanted low ceilings and stopped up short, feeling Reese's presence behind her. "These would be the children's rooms," she said quietly.

Reese made a sound in his throat. "Don't think so."

She whirled around too quickly and nearly bumped his chest. "I thought you wanted children," she said without thinking.

Reese stared down into her eyes, and for a long moment he didn't say a word. Then finally he said, "*Wanted* is the correct word."

As in past tense.

Reese had wanted children; they both had. And when they'd been together they'd daydreamed about having them and how their world would change.

Eliza turned around to glance at the attic bedrooms that may never hear a child's laughter. "I still want them," she admitted, unable to choke back her wistful tone.

But when she turned around, Reese had moved down the hallway to the sitting room.

After Eliza had seen every room in the house, she

gazed out the kitchen window, staring at the skyline, where the treetops met the Montana sky. It truly was big-sky country, beautiful and wide and remote. Eliza felt it all, and suddenly loneliness as vast and simple as the land itself claimed her. She let out a breathy sigh. "You have the bare bones of a gorgeous home, Reese."

He stood behind her, and she took in the scent of him, all crispness and pine, and yearned for things she hadn't dared in a very long time.

"I know."

"And a lot of decisions to make."

"A lot."

"You can afford the best decorators in the world. So why am I here?" she asked.

He wrapped his arms around her, pressing her back to his chest. But that move also placed her rear end in between his hips, the taut, firm length of him meshing with her.

She squeezed her eyes shut.

"I wanted to get you alone," he said, shoving her hair aside to nibble on her throat.

She arched into the soft, tender kisses. "But…you're angry with me."

"Furious."

He continued kissing her throat while the hands that wrapped around her waist climbed higher, to spread out just under her breasts.

She held her breath. "We're getting divorced."

"That's a fact."

His thumbs lifted to flick the crest of her breasts, the tiny act causing a riot to her system.

A loud thunderous clap brought both their heads up. Menacing black clouds moved in quickly, the sky now dark with the threat of a storm.

"Damn it," Reese said, breaking away from her. "It's gonna be a soaker! Grab your things. We'll make a run for it."

But before Eliza could grasp what was happening, Reese had tossed her jacket to her, slapped the Stetson on her head, picked up her briefcase and slid his hand in hers. "Let's go."

"Where?" she asked as he tugged her to the back door of the house.

"The cottage." And they made a dash toward the structure Eliza hadn't noticed before. The quaint one-level cottage nestled behind the house and closer to the lake was at least half a football field away.

Reese held her hand tight and she pushed herself to keep pace. The air outside hit her with chilling force, so much colder now than when they'd first arrived. Overhead the clouds opened up, bursting with sound and might, drenching them with blinding, merciless rain.

And in an instant the rain became hailstones, hitting them hard, then pinging onto the ground. Once they finally made it to the cottage, Reese guided her inside and released her hand, heading for the fireplace. "At least we have electricity in here. I'll turn on the heat in a sec, but a fire will warm us up faster. We should probably get out of these wet clothes."

Eliza blinked, watching him throw logs into the fireplace. "Even the weather cooperates with you, Reese."

Reese turned around and the dimple peeked out from

his crooked smile. "I can't take credit for the storm, darlin', but I don't think I could've planned this any better," he said without apology. "Looks like snow's on the way."

Snow?

Eliza knew what that meant.

"You're gonna have to stay the night."

Six

Reese built the fire up until the small living room glowed with golden firelight and heat sliced through the cold air. On bended knee, he glanced at Eliza shivering by the hearth, her hands jutting out toward the warmth.

"I can't stay here tonight," she said. "I have to get home."

"I doubt anyone's flying out anywhere today. Take off your wet clothes, Eliza. You're chilled to the bone."

She shuddered. "I'm…fine. The fire will dry me."

Reese stood. "Suit yourself." He took his jacket off, then unbuttoned his shirt and tossed it aside. "I'm not gonna freeze my butt off just because you decided to get modest on me."

With that, he stretched his T-shirt over his head and

flung that, too. When he went for his belt buckle, Eliza gasped, "Reese!"

"What?" he said, ready to yank off the belt. He watched Eliza's blue eyes round on his chest before lifting up to face him.

"Do you…uh, have anything else for me to wear?"

He nodded. "I'll find you something. Hang on. I'll be right back."

"You have women's clothes here?" she asked just before he stepped out the door.

"Wait and see," he replied without missing stride.

And when he returned with a black velour robe and one of his flannel shirts, Eliza lifted one blond brow.

"My father lived here with me. What'd you think?"

Eliza took the offered clothes without commenting. "I'll just use your bathroom to put these on."

"No, change in here. It's warmer. I'll make coffee. And we'll see about drying your clothes."

Ten minutes later Reese returned to the fire wearing a dry pair of jeans and a shirt, holding two mugs of steaming hot coffee. Eliza sat with her legs folded under her, cuddled up in his robe. Her hair was still slightly damp, spread out over the collar, catching firelight. "It's snowing."

"Hmm. A good day to be inside." He handed her the mug, then sat beside her in front of the fire.

"Thanks," she said, her face downcast. "I guess I'm not getting out today."

"Is that what you really want?"

Her blue eyes widened for a sec, before she took a deep breath. "I'm not sure what I want."

She stood then, and Reese made note of bright

purple painted toenails peeking out from his robe, so unlike the prissy socialite and so reminiscent of the woman he'd married.

He sipped his coffee, watching her roam around the room. "How long did your father live here?"

"About six months. He liked it here, didn't want any part of the big house."

"It's cozy," she said. "But very masculine. Big beams. Stone fireplace. Lots of wood everywhere. But there's charm here, too. Must have been hard when he died."

"Can't deny that."

"Did you have help when you packed up his things?"

Reese swallowed and didn't respond.

She looked down at him. "You haven't?"

He rubbed the back of his neck. "Not yet."

"There's time," she said gently. "My father said that when my mother died, he couldn't face packing up anything of hers. Everything remained as it was for a very long time, until finally two of his best friends came over and told him it was time. They helped him get through it."

Reese sipped more of his coffee. He wasn't sure he was ready for that.

"If you could come up with some boxes, I wouldn't mind helping," she said. "I mean, we might have all day with nothing else to—"

"Let me think about it," he said, touched by her offer to help. But he'd be damned doing any such thing with her. Not when she looked the way she did, naked underneath his robe, her hair shimmering in the firelight and her purple toenails driving him crazy.

"Okay," she said softly. Then she wandered over to

the bookshelves and lifted up one of his championship rodeo buckles. "I remember when you won this," she whispered before setting it back in place.

He rose to stand beside her. "I remember how we celebrated. In the cab of my truck. Couldn't wait to get home. We were all over each other."

She slid her eyes closed and took a long breath. When she opened them, blue flames of desire seared into his.

He untied her robe and slipped his hands inside, splaying them around her waist. "You always did look great wearing my shirts."

"Reese," she said, a warning note in her voice.

"Damn it, we're still married." He brought his lips down on hers, taking her in a long, heady kiss. She made little throaty sounds that stirred him up, and he deepened the kiss until both were breathless and turned on when it ended. "You're my wife."

"Not for long," she whispered.

"For now." And he kissed her again, tucking his hands around her backside, bringing her flush with his body. "Don't deny what you want, Eliza. We both know I'm gonna lay you down by that fire and make love to you." For hours, into the night, until he could put her out of his mind for good.

He was in lust with his wife. Once he satisfied that craving, he would finally move on, leaving her behind—the way she did him six years ago.

Eliza couldn't deny she wanted him. There hadn't been anyone else in all this time, and Reese was here, wanting her, making her body tingle and her heartbeat quicken. So when he took her hand, she followed him and together they lay down by the fire, the plush robe under her serving as their bed. Reese wasted no time unbuttoning the shirt she wore and spreading the material, exposing every inch of her.

He rose up on his knees between her legs, a look of admiration in his eyes, and on a deep breath he said, "Just as sexy as I remember."

She felt exposed and vulnerable for a moment, but his expression never wavered. Desire burned deep in his eyes as he slowly unbuttoned his shirt, exposing a darkly tanned, muscled torso. Eliza watched, unguarded now, unable to tear her gaze away. He removed his belt and buckle and, keeping his jeans on, pressed his body over hers. His lips met hers and she breathed him in, his all-male scent, delighted that he'd remembered how she liked the rough slide of his jeans on her body.

He kissed her deeply, mating his tongue with hers in an openmouthed, hot, lusty frenzy. His lips moved over her, touching her everywhere and he made love to the whole of her body first, making her ache so deeply that she felt the pain of it down to her core.

But it was his words, whispered seductively in her ear, commanding her touch and telling her in more than sensual terms what he wanted to do and how he would do it, that affected her most. Those lusty words echoed in her mind, and Reese's quiet declarations turned her body to searing lava, an eruption that readied to flow. She was hot, melting, primed for him to take her, Reese's brand of foreplay never failing to saturate her with sizzling heat.

She reached for the snap of his jeans, lowered the zipper and touched where he wanted to be touched, where she *longed* to touch.

"Still magic," he rasped out as she continued to stroke him until both needed more. He moved her hands aside and joined their bodies in a long-awaited reunion. Skin to skin now, rough to smooth, he moved over her, with her, inside her, until the years faded away and she was with him wholly now, completely.

"Let go, baby," he commanded gently. "Hold nothing back."

And Eliza flew, her body releasing with overpowering force. She clenched and moaned with pleasure over and over until she trembled with completion.

She knew Reese held back, his stamina and endurance something deliciously wicked. And they made love again and again, until the raging fire in the hearth died down to serene simmering embers.

If the third time's the charm, then Eliza had been thoroughly, unmistakably, unbelievably charmed.

All three times.

Exhausted, spent and fully satisfied, she cuddled against Reese and fell fast asleep.

Eliza sat on the sofa facing the fire, glancing at Reese as he slept. Outside, falling snow made a pretty picture, frosting the leaves with white flakes and dusting the landscape with loose powder. The cold winter scene outside distinctly contrasted with the cozy temperatures inside the cottage.

She wore her clothes, soft and warm from the dryer,

as she worked up her own sketches of Reese's home. Now that she'd seen the rooms firsthand, she had a better understanding of how each room should flow into the next with colors, textures and style.

The house was unique, in a class all its own—not unlike Reese, who would soon move in and set roots down for the first time in his life.

He'd changed quite a bit in six years, she'd recognized, but he still had the ability to flame her body. Her long, dry drought was finally over, and she'd made up her mind to live in the moment, to simply enjoy rather than think of any repercussions.

"Don't think I'm through with you yet," he'd whispered gently right before they'd fallen asleep in each other's arms. Eliza had slept with a smile on her face, grateful that Reese was an insatiable lover.

As long as she didn't fall in love with him again, she'd be fine.

They'd been careful. Reese had taken the proper precautions. They were still married, so why shouldn't she enjoy a healthy, thoroughly satisfying sexual interlude?

With her husband.

Reese's low voice startled her. "You look busy."

"You're awake."

"Barely," he said, rolling onto his back to stare at the rough beam ceiling. "What time is it?"

"Four."

His chest was bare, and he'd slept with his jeans riding low on his hips, the snap opened enough for her to view his navel and then some. He rolled onto his side, his hand bracing his head, to study her. "What are you working on?"

She snapped her briefcase closed. "Designs. I'll show you later. Do you have anything to eat in this house?"

Reese chuckled. "Sex always did make you hungry," he said, then added more wistfully, "I forgot that." He rose and stretched, pulling his muscles taut, lifting his arms up high in the air. Then he turned to toss a few logs on the fire before adding, "You got dressed."

"I can't roam around all day in your…shirt."

He shot her a no-nonsense look. "Why not?"

"I really am hungry, Reese."

"I noticed." His mouth twitched.

"For *food* this time."

Rising, he strode over to her, bent down and kissed her lightly on the lips. "Okay, let's see what's cooking in the kitchen."

It was so casual a kiss, so off-the-cuff, so reminiscent of their life together back when things were carefree and easy, that Eliza froze. She sat ramrod stiff, chastising herself for thinking the unthinkable.

She *couldn't* fall in love with him again. They were getting a divorce. They'd moved on, leading separate lives now. She wouldn't even think about the out-and-out lies she'd told her family.

"You coming?" he called out.

She shoved the briefcase and those thoughts aside and walked into the kitchen. "Neither one of us can cook worth a darn. Too bad it's snowing…oh, you have an indoor grill."

Reese pulled two steaks out of the refrigerator. He grabbed two beers, a package of frozen vegetables and some sourdough bread and set them on the table. "Between the two of us, we can rig something up."

Eliza's stomach growled. "If you can manage not to burn the steaks, I'll do the rest."

"I never burn the steaks," he said in a serious tone.

"You always burn the steaks."

"We never had steak," he said defiantly.

Eliza stopped for a moment, then conceded the point. "You always burned the *burgers*."

With a quick nod, Reese admitted, "That's better."

They ate partially burned steaks with overcooked and underseasoned veggies, but at least the bread was fresh and the beer cold. After the meal, Eliza pulled out her drawings and they sat comfortably on the sofa, going over her ideas.

Reese sipped from his second beer, watching her eyes skim over the layouts he had stashed here in the cottage. She'd marked them up with her design ideas, and he had to admit they were good.

"The windows downstairs that look out onto the lake shouldn't be covered. The view is breathtaking. You wouldn't want to hide that, unless of course you want—"

"I don't," he interrupted. "I agree. Keep them uncovered."

She smiled and nodded. "I see deep hues of golds and browns in the living rooms. The great room with a stacked stone fireplace should have built-in shelves on each side—pine would work nicely. And the floor should be all wood, with some woven carpets to break it up. I've written it all down."

"Okay," he agreed. Damn if he couldn't picture the rooms taking shape the way she described them.

She nodded again and continued to work through the drawings. "In the sky bedrooms I see blue. Blue walls and whitewashed wood trim all over. There's this great color called Blue Bliss—I think it'd be perfect."

"Okay," he said, continuing to watch her. She really loved this work, yet she spent her time on fund-raising. Not that helping charities wasn't noble, but he knew she wasn't doing what was in her heart. Reese thought it had something to do with her family and their attitude toward her craft. They supported her home projects, but never believed she'd make a success of herself if she branched out in the world. That was part of Eliza's problem, he thought. She didn't have enough faith in herself. And she certainly hadn't placed any faith in their marriage.

Her eyes glowed with passion now and Reese hid a satisfied grin. He'd seen that same look on her face hours ago, when they'd exhausted each other. He liked that Eliza liked having sex. It had sure made being married to her a hell of a lot of fun. But having sex and making love were two different things. They'd had wild, uninhibited, mind-blowing sex today, a release of pent-up tension for her and total frustration for him. Tonight, he planned on taking her to his bed and making slow, easy, lazy love to her. He wanted to draw out the pleasure for as long as he could. For both of them.

He'd half hoped that taking her to bed wouldn't

have been as good, as thrilling as it once was, but it had been that and more. It hadn't been exactly the same but even better.

Which would make saying goodbye to her that much harder. But there was no doubt in his mind that they had to part ways. Still furious with her, still pissed off at how easily she'd thrown away their marriage, thinking that he'd been unfaithful to her, Reese couldn't find the forgiveness he needed. He'd clung to his fury too long to let a roll or two in the sack change his mind.

Yet, as he watched her work so diligently, with her head down and all that glossy blond hair falling across her shoulders, he couldn't deny that he wanted her. When he'd fallen in love with her, it'd been a hard fall. He'd had to pick himself up by the bootstraps to get on with his life when she'd left him. And he had. There was no turning back.

"So what do you want to do in the master bedroom?" she asked.

That question grabbed his attention. "Get naked again?"

She blushed, her pretty face going all rosy. "Reese, be serious. I'm talking about your new master bedroom."

"I *am* being serious."

She glanced down at the designs in her lap. "But… we have more to do."

He stood and gathered up the layouts, tossing them onto the sofa, then reached for her hand. He tugged her up so that she stood toe-to-toe with him. "I'm glad you agree."

Bending his head, he kissed her soundly on the lips.

When she gazed into his eyes with dewy softness, Reese lifted her up into his arms. "Let's go check out my bedroom. See if you can make any improvements in there."

Reese lowered her down onto his bed and took his time with her, creating a slow, tortuous buildup of desire. Eliza wove her hands in his short sandy locks, explored his shoulders and his back while he kissed her, caressed her skin, nibbled on her body, making her moan with easy, unhurried pleasure.

He moistened her breasts with his tongue until she ached, then slid his hands down to her belly, making circles in slow motion until he reached farther down to cup her womanhood. She arched up quickly.

"Relax, baby," he whispered in her ear. "You won't be sorry."

And she did relax, letting her body succumb to all the things Reese did to her, all the things he whispered in her ear.

They moved erotically, in rhythm with each other. And when he rolled onto his back, Eliza took him in her hand, then her mouth and wrung out the pleasure for him the way he had for her.

And, once protected, Reese rasped, "Show me how it's done." Eliza felt no shame, completely wrapped up in the moment as she recalled this command—their private little joke from Reese's rodeo days.

Eliza climbed atop and took him in, moving on him with undulations that created a lusty, sexy ride for both. She reveled in the pleasure on his face as she rode the wave, and when he took control, guiding her with his hands and hips, she moved quicker now, sensations heightened, meeting his powerful thrusts until both shuddered with striking force.

Minutes later, cradled in Reese's arms, she spoke from her heart. "I never minded burgers, Reese."

Reese's chest heaved and he blew out that breath slowly. "I shouldn't have married you, Eliza. I was outclassed and I knew it. I couldn't provide you with what you needed."

"Reese," she said, turning to look into his eyes, "it was never about money."

It was about love, and they had that. They'd fallen in love quickly, madly and had been crazy about each other. When she believed he'd been unfaithful, the wound to her heart had been devastating. She'd been injured beyond belief and had to go home to Sioux Falls and pretend everything was right in her life. Whenever someone had caught her with a distant, remote look on her face, they'd simply blamed Warren Keyes and the scandal of their broken engagement. But Warren had been the last thing on her mind. She'd been filled with Reese Parker and she'd lost him.

"We had burgers in the kitchen, but *steak* in the bedroom," she added.

Reese shoved up from the bed and peered down at her. "Yeah, the sex was hot. Still is. But you couldn't bring yourself to tell your family about me. Then or now."

He stood up and nailed her with a hard look. "And then you walked out on me thinking I'd cheated on you. Guess you never really knew me, Eliza."

She watched him walk into the bathroom, heard the

shower turn on and knew he would wash away what had happened between them just now and cling to his righteous anger.

That night, Reese held Eliza close, breathing in her scent, reminded of her gentle moves and little sounds she made as she slept. He managed to shove all thoughts of her betrayal out of his mind so that he could get a decent night's sleep. As it turned out, he'd never slept better.

Morning dawned, and with the storm over, the sun breaking through lingering clouds, Reese rose quietly, leaving Eliza in his bed. He dressed and entered the room in the back of the cottage he'd converted into a temporary office to make some business calls.

After two long-winded conversations that sapped his energy, he hung up the phone, leaned back in his chair and stared out the window. He'd never liked the business end of the oil business. It made him antsy and impatient. He'd much rather be out in the field, working with his experienced crew—the roughnecks who knew everything there was to know about drilling oil—seeing firsthand when a well blew, streaming rich black crude. And though he hadn't enjoyed becoming a suit, he'd loved every second of his success, building a company from the ground up, employing dozens of workers, being in control of his life.

He'd never give up that control again.

Eliza's bright laughter broke through his thoughts. Suppressing a smile, he walked down the hallway toward the sound to see what his soon-to-be ex was doing.

He found her in the kitchen.

In another man's arms.

The jar to his system staggered him momentarily.

Until he realized she was dancing with his brother, Garrett.

Dancing?

"Hey, look who decided to crawl out of his hole this morning." Garrett stopped long enough to slant him a big smile.

Reese leaned against the doorjamb, arms crossed, irritated at the jealous sweep of emotion that invaded him. "Hands off, little brother."

Garrett's smile never faded, but he did release Eliza, lifting his hands in the air, palms up in old Western-movie-style. "I was only showing the lady the two-step."

"I was just telling Garrett I've got a fund-raiser coming up this spring and I needed a refresher course in—"

"What are you doing here?" Reese asked his brother, none too pleased seeing the rosy glow of joy on Eliza's face, a glow his *brother* had put there. This time the stab he felt pissed him off big-time.

"Just checking on your property, bro. After the snow-storm, I thought I'd see if the house was still standing." He winked at Eliza and she grinned. "Little did I know I'd find my sister-in-law here."

She had showered and dressed. Eggs were frying in a pan and coffee brewed in the pot. Reese pushed away from the door and entered the kitchen, grabbing a mug and pouring a cup of coffee. "We're going over the terms of our divorce."

Garrett lifted his brows.

Color drained from Eliza's face.

Reese sipped his coffee.

"And I thought you brought Eliza here to give you ideas about the house." Garrett glanced at her and she sent him a shaky smile.

"Is that what you thought?" He spoke to Garrett and then winced inwardly seeing Eliza turn quickly away. In that fleeting moment, he noted her every emotion—hurt, anger, betrayal and dawning realization—register on her face. Reese sucked in a deep breath. "Fire the decorator. She's all wrong. I'll find someone else."

Garrett shook his head. "You hired her. You're gonna have to let her go."

Reese nodded, conceding the point. "You're right."

"He hates it when I'm right," Garrett said to Eliza. She was busy scrambling eggs. She glanced up and their eyes met for an instant. She stabbed at the eggs, the spatula making mincemeat of them, and Reese figured she'd imagined the eggs were his head as she smashed his brains into tiny pieces.

Hell, he'd wanted to get his revenge. He'd wanted to tempt her with this house, show her what she'd thrown away, injure her the way she had him…and he'd succeeded. But he wasn't ready to let her go.

"It's time I got going," Garrett said.

"Me, too," Eliza said, piercing Reese with a look. "I want to go home."

"Done," he said. "My pilot is on standby."

"Then, if you'll excuse me, I have a phone call to

make." With that, Eliza breezed past him and left him alone with Garrett.

Garrett poked a fork into the eggs, sampling them. "You sure you know what you're doing, Reese?"

Reese narrowed his eyes. "I always know what I'm doing."

His brother chewed for a moment, then set his fork down and shot him a look. Hell, he hated when Garrett got serious. "So you're through punishing her?"

"Sleeping with my wife would hardly be considered… punishment. Didn't get a single complaint last night." Reese finished off his coffee.

"That's not what I meant and you know it." Garrett lowered his voice, glancing toward the hallway. "She said she offered to help you pack up Pops's things."

"She told you that between dances?"

"We had a little conversation about Pops, yeah. It was damn nice of her, Reese. She's a keeper. And if you're too stubborn to see it, then quit messing with her. Let her go."

"When I'm ready."

"Oh, you're ready, brother. In fact, if she has anything to say about it, right about now…you're *toast*."

Seven

"I can't thank you enough, Eliza," Diana said as they folded up Diana's summer clothes to ship off to Australia. "This is hardly as easy as packing up my stuff from Wellesley."

Eliza smiled, remembering her college days with Diana. Her beautiful bedroom was ten times the size of their room in the sorority house. "You mean when all we had was half a closetful of clothes, our books and some videos?"

"Don't forget the posters of Bon Jovi. We *both* had plenty of those."

"I remember. I think I still have them somewhere," Eliza said, trying to keep her focus. She'd offered to help Diana pack up her house, boxing up some things for Max to take with him to Australia. But in truth,

Eliza's heart wasn't in it. She'd been distracted ever
since Reese put her on his private jet alone, sending her
back to Sioux Falls, three days ago. He'd claimed he
was needed in Montana and had provided her with
the plane trip, a limo to take her home and a long goodbye kiss.

Or kiss-off.

She'd had one glorious day and night with Reese,
before it had all fallen apart. Now she was angrier than
she'd ever been—at herself…and at Reese. She'd
fallen into his trap. She realized that now. Reese had
wanted to tempt her with that stunning house, his
success, the man he'd become. She'd seen it all…and
she could envision a life with him again. But then
suddenly he'd pulled the rug out from under her and
had given her the brush-off.

She fully expected to receive the divorce papers by
messenger now, the final blow to a marriage that should
never have occurred. It was a mistake to have gotten
involved with him again. She should have insisted on
signing the divorce papers as soon as he'd shown up on
her doorstep. Now, she realized, as the ache in the pit of
her stomach would testify, she still had feelings for him.
If she didn't, husband or not, she would never have slept
with him again. That whole day had been magical. At
least *she'd* thought so. But for Reese it had only been a
game. She didn't know what he truly wanted from her.
At one time he'd been a person she could trust and rely
on. She'd had so few people in her life that she could
really depend on, and Diana, her dear friend who would
be leaving for Australia soon, was one of them.

"Oh, look, I still have the ticket stub for the... Hey, Eliza, what's wrong?" Diana asked softly. "You've been staring off into space since you got here this morning."

Eliza wouldn't lie. Not to Diana. She was sick of lying to her friends. "I know. I'm sorry." She folded up the box she'd just filled with summer shorts and tank tops and turned to her friend. "Remember when I told you that I've been keeping a secret for a long time?"

Diana's gray-green eyes widened with surprise. "I do, but you never told me what it was about."

"Well, it's about Reese Parker."

"The gorgeous guy who came to dinner the other night?"

Eliza nodded. "We have a past."

"Oh, well...he did seem to have a connection to you. But, honestly, I thought he was someone you'd just met. I caught him looking at you a few times during dinner. And I thought, oh, boy, this guy's interested in Eliza."

Eliza sighed and sat down on Diana's bed. She picked up a ruffled pillow and hugged it to her chest. "It's a long story, but basically my life's in limbo right now. I spent some time with him again...and, well, I thought we were through. Now I'm not sure what to think."

"He lives in Montana?"

She nodded.

"That shouldn't be a problem. Look how I met Max. And now I'm getting married and moving to Australia. Montana seems doable."

"It's not where he lives that's the problem. It seems neither one of us can move on from what happened in our past. We're both...angry. I'm not sure I can trust him."

"Wow—sounds familiar."

Eliza smiled and took her friend's hand. She couldn't help but envy Diana for the way her life had worked out. She'd had her problems with Max, but they'd been resolved and now Diana had a wonderful life ahead of her. Eliza felt that maybe her chance with Reese had come and gone six years ago. "I'm happy for you. You know that. Max is wonderful and you're going to have a great life with him. But for me, I'm afraid to hope for that kind of happiness. I have a good life. I don't want you to think I'm whining, but there's always been something missing."

"Because you never knew your mother?"

"Yes, that's part of it. I think I'd be able to confide in my mother the way some moms and daughters talk. I really miss that. Patricia seems so moody lately, but we've never been very close anyway. My father and brothers love me, I know that. But I've never felt as close to another human being as I was with Reese. We spent one whole summer together right after my break-up with Warren. It was the best time in my life. And then everything fell apart."

"Wow. You were in love with him."

"Deeply."

"What are you going to do?" Diana asked with sympathy in her eyes.

"I'm going to concentrate on the Children's Center fund-raiser coming up next month. I've got loads of work to do and I'm hoping to put Reese Parker completely out of my mind."

She grabbed another box and starting filling it with

yearbooks, photo albums and CDs. "But first I'm going to pack you up and get you ready for your trip. And then you're taking me out to lunch."

Diana chuckled. "That was the deal."

"Yes, and there's no backing out on a deal."

Eliza had never backed out on a commitment in her life. Ending her marriage would be a first.

And it meant losing Reese all over again.

Reese glanced down at the papers piling up on his desk and frowned. He'd been swamped with work and had yet to get away from his three-story office building any earlier than ten o'clock at night in the last few days. He had reports to read, permits to file and Leanne's latest geology survey waiting for him to go over. Garrett sat facing him with an expectant look, waiting for an answer about whether to abandon Well #13, the directional drilling project that had run into costly problems.

When his secretary buzzed in, Reese pushed the intercom button, grunting at her, "What?"

"Sorry to interrupt, Reese, but I've got another decorator lined up. She'll meet you at your house at five this afternoon."

Reese ran a hand through his hair. Hell, he didn't want to see another damn decorator. None of the three he'd already met with had been right. He couldn't trust them with his house. "Can't make it."

"How about—"

"No. Put them all on hold for now, Sally. It's a waste of my time. I don't like any of them. It'll just have to wait."

"Okay, let me know when you have time."

"I will," he said, and as an apology for his foul mood he added with more civility, "Thank you, Sally. I appreciate it."

"Sure, boss."

Then he faced Garrett. "So the whipstocking didn't pan out? I think we should abandon the well. No sense pouring good money after bad. But before we do, let's check with Leanne, okay?"

Garrett nodded, his eyes going just a little bright at the mention of their geologist's name. Garrett had it bad for the brown-eyed brunette who had just as much brains as good looks, even behind those black-rimmed eyeglasses she wore. She'd been a godsend to them both, her intelligence matching up with Garrett's hands-on approach and Reese's good instincts. Together they made a great team and a whole lot of money. But Garrett, never one to be shy, was out of his element with her.

"Okay. But I'm with you. No sense throwing more money into that well. We've had too many problems as it is. And speaking of problems, I take it you're not getting anywhere with your house?"

"No." Reese didn't want to delve too deeply into his reasons for turning down four decorators already. None compared to Eliza. He hadn't gotten her off his mind for more than a few minutes at a time during his very busy days. He had more thinking to do and didn't want to discuss her with anyone, not even his brother.

Garrett sat there smiling and nodding his head.

Reese ignored him and looked down at the reports on his desk. "Anything else?"

"Yeah, something else. She got under your skin, didn't she?"

Reese wouldn't feign ignorance. He knew what his brother was getting at. "Like a thorn."

"So you're still bleeding?"

"No! I'm not bleeding, Garrett." Reese let out an impatient sigh.

"Are you or are you not getting a divorce?" Garrett asked.

"None of your damn business."

"My brother's happiness is my business," Garrett bantered back easily. "And I think you still care about her."

The truth was that Reese had been having second thoughts about Eliza. All he'd wanted for six years was to get even with her, to pay her back for the heartache she'd caused him. He'd accomplished what he'd set out to do, but being with her again had been…incredible. He'd been with women in the past and there hadn't been a one that measured up to her. All short-term casual affairs that meant nothing to him. But Eliza had meant something. At one time she'd been everything to him.

He'd struggled these past few days with his need for revenge. When he'd kissed her goodbye the other day at the airport, she'd been rightfully angry with him. He'd deliberately hurt her and she'd known it. The brush-off had been complete. But as he'd stood on the tarmac watching the plane take off, taking Eliza away from him for good, he'd wondered if he'd done the right thing.

She'd explained her reasons for leaving him six years

ago, and deep down Reese knew that Eliza had known very little love in her life. She'd *never* known complete unconditional binding love, so maybe she hadn't been able to recognize it when she'd experienced it with him. She hadn't trusted him. She should have, but could he overlook that now? Could he even begin to forgive her?

She'd been caught between a stepmother who hadn't shown her great affection, an indifferent father and two brothers who had their own lives to live. Her family was a mess, in his estimation. The powerful Fortunes were hardly the picture-perfect family the press would have people believe. They had problems, hardships, secrets and scandals.

The more he thought about her, the more he realized he had to make sure before letting her go. He had to see her one more time.

But he sure as hell wouldn't give his brother the satisfaction of being right. "Let it be, Garrett. I'm not in the mood."

Garrett scoffed. "You're fooling your—"

Leanne walked in, glancing down at the files she was holding. "Sorry to interrupt, boys, but I need a minute of your time."

Reese rose from his chair, shoving files into his briefcase as inspiration struck. One way to keep Garrett out of his hair was to put him in the hot seat. "You know what, Leanne, you can discuss anything you need to with Garrett. You two…work together. I'm beat. I'm taking this work home. You both know how to reach me in case of an emergency."

He walked out with the satisfying image of two very stunned expressions in his wake.

"Thanks for getting me away from work today, Nic. I haven't had a girls' day out in quite some time. Lunch and a shopping spree really helped." Eliza climbed the steps to her house, carrying three shopping bags full of new clothes, lingerie and shoes. She'd gone all out and a little wild with Roberto Cavalli, Dolce & Gabbana and Prada today.

"You've earned a little indulgence, Eliza. It's been a heck of a week for you," Nicole said, removing her Christian Dior sunglasses as they entered the sunlit foyer. "And I'm not just speaking about the Children's Center fund-raiser you're organizing. You've been on a roller-coaster ride this week." Then, lowering her voice and speaking near Eliza's ear, she added, "With your blockhead of a husband."

Eliza chuckled. No one who'd ever seen Reese or spent any time with him would ever consider him a blockhead. Yet she'd come up with a few choice descriptive words for him lately, as well. "I can't think about him, Nic," she said. "It's too darn confusing."

But she had thought about him every single day. And at night, while trying to sleep, his image would appear and she'd recall that one blissful snowcapped day they'd spent in Montana. For a short time, Reese had let down his guard, showing her the man he'd once been, the man she had once loved so desperately.

He'd been sweet and strong when they'd made love as though the past six bitter years had simply faded away.

Eliza smiled at the memory of being in his arms and feeling his power and tenderness, his fierce desire and his unshielded passion. Nothing had ever been better.

But he'd hurt her and she still reeled from that unexpected rejection. Even one week later, Eliza felt the cold slap of his calculated rebuff.

She should feel relieved that he was gone once again from her life. Her secret marriage was safe and would soon end. But she had a niggling feeling that he wasn't through with her yet. And that she wouldn't like what else he had planned for her.

"Confusing or not, you're holding up better than I would under the circumstances."

"Looks like you two girls did some damage today." Nash Fortune walked into the foyer, looking over Eliza's shopping bags.

"Hi, Dad."

"Hello, Mr. Fortune," Nic said. "Nice to see you."

"It's always good to see you, Nicole. So what have you two been doing besides emptying out the boutiques?"

Nic laughed. "That just about covers it. That and a gourmet lunch at the Culver Hotel."

"Eliza, I can't recall the last time you've been on a shopping spree," her dad said, wearing a curious expression.

"I twisted her arm," Nic offered, "and she twisted mine. I've got *five* shopping bags sitting in my car."

Nash looked at Nicole with a smile and a shake of his head, then directed his attention to Eliza, raising an eyebrow. "Does all this shopping have anything to do with Reese Parker?"

Eliza glanced at her friend and then, on a swallow, returned the question. "Why would you think that?"

She'd had enough experience with lying to throw the ball back in her father's court, so to speak. The less she revealed, the better. But she was darn curious to know what her father meant. He hadn't questioned her about her trip to Montana other than asking how her return flight had been after the snowstorm.

"Take a look in the kitchen, honey."

Puzzled, Eliza walked through the foyer and into the great room that led to the kitchen, with Nicole and her father right behind her. Once she stepped into the kitchen, she gasped. "Oh, these are…lovely." She turned back to her father. "Are you saying these are for me?"

Nash pursed his lips. "Patricia doesn't care for tulips. You know she loves roses."

"Right," Eliza said, staring at a huge bouquet of pink, lavender and white tulips sitting tall and pretty in a simple glass vase. With impending dread shoving through her sense of pure delight, she asked, "You didn't read the card, did you, Dad?"

Nash shot her a you-know-me-better-than-that look. "No. But a man can assume, can't he? He flew you to Montana, honey. It doesn't take a rocket scient—"

"That was business, Dad," she interrupted as she touched the firm, smooth petal of one of the flowers.

Her father scoffed gently, with an incredulous note in his voice. "Are you saying he's actually going to hire you?"

Eliza's stomach churned, both from her father's lack of faith in her and from Reese's obvious attempt to throw temptation at her with a house any decorator would love to get their hands on. Obviously neither of them thought her worthy of the challenge.

She managed a slight shrug in answer.

"Must be three dozen there," Nic said, changing the subject. "They are gorgeous."

"Mmm," Eliza said, removing the card nestled between the tall stems. Tulips had special meaning for her, and damn Reese for remembering. For making her think about the mare named Tulip and that one wild, sensual ride they'd both taken that day in the saddle.

From then on, tulips had been her favorite flower.

It had been their private little joke.

Eliza hated to open the card, but not doing so would only cast more suspicion. She read the card silently. *Remember?* it said. She'd been right—this had been Reese's doing. But the rest of the note caused her more alarm. *Dinner at seven tonight. I'll pick you up.*

She closed the card carefully. "It's just a thank-you for helping him the other day," she fibbed, hating herself for lying and Reese for putting her into this position.

Her father nodded with a dubious expression and bid the girls farewell. "I'll see you later, girls. Eliza, we won't be home for dinner tonight. I think I've just thought up a way to surprise Patricia. And you can thank Parker for that."

Eliza managed a small smile. She hated that her father even knew Reese's name. "Okay, Dad. Have a nice time."

"Goodbye, Mr. Fortune."

As soon as Nash left the kitchen, Nicole lifted wide

eyes to her. "Well? Don't keep me in suspense. What does the note say?"

Eliza handed her the note and she read it aloud. "Remember?" Nicole peered at her waiting for an explanation.

"Don't ask. It's too personal. But he wants to have dinner with me?"

Nicole glanced at the note again. "He's not giving you a choice. This isn't an invitation but a command."

"Yeah, I noticed that. The old Reese wouldn't have been so demanding. He'd have asked me out sweetly and I would have melted from his charm."

"Maybe he's ready to have you sign the divorce papers now."

Eliza pursed her lips. "He doesn't have to deliver them in person. We've, uh, said all there is to say."

Nicole cast her a serious look. "Have you really?"

"Yes, I think so. I can't…do this. I'm not going out with him tonight."

"God, Lizzie. That white Escada outfit you bought today would be perfect."

Eliza rolled her eyes. "Traitor."

"Well, it would be. Don't deny you didn't have a man in mind when you bought that."

"I must have *lost* my mind to let you talk me into it."

"You look great in it."

"Maybe, but I'm not wearing it tonight. If he wants me to sign the divorce papers, I'll do it right here."

"In the house? That's risky."

Eliza let go a pent-up sigh. "I'm tired of lying to everyone, Nic. I just want this to be over. Hopefully I can finally make Reese understand that."

"Are you saying you're over him?"

Eliza's heart sped up thinking of him being back here in Sioux Falls. Thinking of the way it had been with them in the past. Thinking of how they'd spent that one magical night in Montana last week. Was she over Reese? She had to stop lying to herself, as well. "No, I'll never be over him. I love him so much it hurts."

Eight

Early that evening, Eliza changed her clothes, removing her black dress slacks and cashmere sweater in favor of faded blue jeans and a flannel shirt, thinking this the perfect form of rebellion. She would not go out with Reese tonight. She'd stay in, be comfortable in her clothes and work up the designs she had in mind for revamping her bedroom while inside her studio.

When Peggy O'Hare came in a few minutes before seven, Eliza was truly surprised at the hour. She'd finally relaxed enough this afternoon to fully immerse herself in her work, almost forgetting about Reese.

"Sorry to bother you, Eliza. But Mr. Reese Parker is here to see you. I asked him to wait in the great room. Would you care to see him?"

Eliza tidied up her notes and stood. She decided to treat Reese's appearance here tonight in a businesslike manner. They had legal issues to resolve and that was the crux of it. "Yes, I'll be down in a minute. Thanks, Peg."

The aging housekeeper nodded and then smiled. She'd known Eliza since her birth, being a loyal employee and something of a grandmother figure to Eliza, as well. "He's a handsome one," she said. "And quite a bit nicer than that Warren fellow." Peggy wrinkled her nose. "I never liked him."

"Come to think about it, neither did I," Eliza said with a small smile, realizing the great truth in that.

"I'll tell Mr. Parker you'll be down shortly. You'll need a minute to change your clothes."

"No, I won't," Eliza blurted. "I'm coming right down."

Peggy narrowed her eyes but only nodded before exiting the room. She knew Eliza well. On any other occasion, Eliza would never receive a guest in her house without looking her best. But Peggy was never one to pry, thank goodness. It was one reason the entire family trusted her and treated her with respect.

Eager to get this over with, Eliza headed down the grand staircase, finding Reese waiting for her at the base of the stairs. Wearing jeans and a black Western shirt with studded snap buttons, he looked impeccable, gorgeous and just like the old Reese, the one she'd fallen head over heels in love with. He smiled and that darn dimple popped out, making her heart soar. She nearly stumbled on the steps.

Seeing him again affected her more than she wanted to admit.

Good God, he held his black felt Stetson in his hand. She'd always been a sucker for that hat.

"Hello, Eliza," he drawled, the low timbre of his voice setting her nerves on edge.

She reached the bottom stair and took a deep breath. "Reese."

"You got my note?"

Eliza nodded. "Yes. And the flowers," she said without thanking him. "But I'm not going out with you tonight." Or any other night, she thought. She had to make a clean break. Thankfully luck was with her again. The house was seemingly quiet, her father and Patricia out, and heaven knew where everyone else had gone. She could say whatever she needed to without fear.

Reese shot her a quick smile. "Yes, you are."

"No, Reese. Let's just end this now. Did you bring the divorce papers?"

"No."

"No?" Exasperated, Eliza shook her head at him. "Well, you should have. What's going on, Reese? Why are you doing this?"

"I'm taking you out on a date. No great mystery there."

"A date?" Eliza had just about lost all of her patience. She'd never been through a divorce before, but she was reasonably certain you didn't date the husband you'd planned on shedding from your life. "You can't be serious, Reese. What do you really want with me?"

Reese gazed into her eyes, gripped her hips, splaying his hands wide and tugged her closer. He lowered his mouth to hers and claimed her lips in a slow, sensual kiss that knocked Eliza for a loop. She indulged in the familiar taste of him and nestled against his body, breathing in the scent of fresh pine and all man. He consumed her heart and soul, but she couldn't allow it. She had to stop him from destroying what sanity she had left. When she pulled back, he followed, refusing to break off the kiss.

He cupped her head with one hand, while the other kept her close. He dipped his tongue and tasted her, and Eliza's resistance slowly faded away.

When he finally broke away, he stared into her eyes.

"I'm not dressed for a date," she said, and the weak excuse had sounded better in her head.

He glanced at her attire with a leisurely perusal, those dark eyes missing nothing. "You're dressed perfect."

"I can't date you, Reese," she tried again.

"Oh, so you don't really want to learn the two-step?"

"What?" Sharp surprise elevated her voice to a squeak.

He planted a quick kiss on her mouth and laced their hands. "Come on," he said, tugging her along. "I have a warm coat for you in the car. You need your purse or anything?"

Dumbfounded, Eliza shook her head. "No."

Reese seemed to have everything she needed.

"Okay, then I hope those are your dancing shoes, sweetheart."

Eliza glanced down at her Nike Shox. "They'll do," she found herself saying.

Reese escorted her outside, and the chill hit her, immediately knocking sense into her brain.

But it was too late. Reese plopped his Stetson on his

head, then wrapped her inside a suede coat lined with lambswool and ushered her inside his car, heating her body and…warming her heart.

Reese sat back in his seat, sipping Jack Daniel's and Coke, lazily watching Eliza work the dance floor with the instructor he'd hired for the hour. They had the small, trendy honky-tonk to themselves, a three-piece band, full service at the bar and a dining room for the entire evening. As soon as the hour was up, Reese planned on dominating all of Eliza's time.

She had moves. And he liked them all. Even in those plain clothes, the perfection of her curvy body was evident in the flare of her hips in those jeans and the press of plaid against her full breasts. She swayed in rhythm, learning how to shift her weight and rotate around the dance floor with the instructor named Denny Thorpe as her guide.

Reese ached to get her alone again and he didn't know if it annoyed or pleased him that he reacted to her in such a primal way.

She laughed, throwing her head back, apologizing to Denny when she accidentally kicked his shin. Her eyes sparkled blue fire and her face was flushed.

Reese shifted in his seat, uncomfortable with the heat rush invading his groin, and took another swallow of liquor.

When the band stopped playing, Denny released Eliza's hand and faced Reese, the flickering lights traveling the dance floor dotting them with color. "You want a turn now, Mr. Parker?"

"I'll take my turn…later," he said, peering at Eliza. Her face flushed even deeper. "Are you two through?"

Eliza nodded with a breathless smile. "Oh, I think I'm definitely through," she said, looking at Denny. "Thanks for the instruction. It was fun. And I'll contact you about my fund-raiser, okay?"

"Sure. No problem," he said, his spiked hair and tattoos a definite contrast to the posters of Tim and Faith, Toby Keith and Rascal Flatts on the walls at Country Incorporated. Denny didn't look as though he would enjoy country twang, but he'd come highly recommended and had done a great job. "Well, if there's nothing else, I'll be going."

"Thank you," Reese said, standing and tucking a fifty-dollar tip into Denny's hand. "There's nothing else."

And when he left the room, Reese escorted Eliza to her seat. She flopped down ungraciously. "Wow, that was…exhausting."

"You'll get your second wind after dinner."

Eliza pushed her bangs out of her eyes and redid her ponytail, tying up the ends that had fallen down. She glanced at the band, playing a catchy tune, and the team of bartenders and waitresses who were standing by, enjoying the music. "I still can't believe you rented this whole place out."

Reese took his seat, as well. "You said you needed to learn the two-step. You looked good out there."

"Denny's a good instructor. I'm pretty clumsy on the dance floor. I think his shin is still smarting."

Reese smiled, enjoying the carefree banter. He'd been so doggone consumed with revenge that he hadn't taken the time to really enjoy anything in the past. And now he planned on enjoying Eliza, wispy bangs, baby blues, mind-numbing tight jeans and all. "You're mind's always working, isn't it? You suckered that guy in for one of your charity events."

Contrite, Eliza replied, "He offered."

Reese raised his brows.

"Okay, I sort of guilted him into it, but it's for a good cause. While the Sioux Falls' Gentlemen's Club is having a Texas Hold 'Em tournament, the Ladies' Auxiliary will learn the two-step from Denny and a few of his friends."

"And this is to raise money for?"

"The Children's Center. We supply critically ill children with…hope," she said, then added, "last year we built a playground for the kids, provided means of transportation for the families and sent twenty children to Disney World. It was quite a year."

"Would you miss it if you didn't have that in your life anymore?"

Eliza glanced off for a moment, then returned to him with an honest reply. "I'll always volunteer. I've been doing this too long not to. I want to help, but no, I wouldn't miss organizing the events. It's what I do and I do it well. People know that. They're always coming to me and sometimes, Reese, I wish I could just… disappear."

"Then you should."

Eliza chuckled. "It's not that simple."

No, nothing in their lives was simple right now, but Reese never let anyone prod him into doing something that his gut told him not to do. He just wasn't made that way. But for Eliza it was different. She needed that work to fill a void in her life. And to some degree it did fulfill her. Reese couldn't help wondering if Eliza had been searching for something her whole life. Love, maybe? To be accepted and loved for herself? Her lack of faith and trust in him might have had to do with the way she'd been raised—with a silver spoon right out of the dishwasher, instead of one rubbed with love and polished to a shine.

Reese let the subject drop and focused on the meal the waitress had just set before them.

They dined on thinly sliced steak slathered in barbecue sauce, corn on the cob, peanut coleslaw and biscuits. Eliza drank lemonade, while Reese sipped his whiskey and Coke. Eliza nibbled on her food delicately—once a lady, as they say. She'd always been a class act, refined and mannerly.

Except in the bedroom.

There, Eliza threw refinement and inhibition to the wind. She was a wildcat, responsive and sensitive to his every touch. Reese itched to take her to bed again.

She was the only woman he wanted in his bed. He wondered if it were even possible to regain what they once had. So much time had gone by, and hard, angry feelings had been harbored on both ends for all of that time.

Eliza played with the remaining food on her plate, moving her fork around. When she finally glanced up, he noted indecision in her eyes. "So why are we on this date? And don't say it's because I needed to learn the two-step."

Reese leaned back in his seat and studied her, deciding to grant her the truth. Maybe it was time for both of them to come clean. "Were you ever going to tell your family about our marriage, Eliza?"

Her blue eyes went wide with shock. She leaned back in her seat slowly, setting her napkin on the table with care. "Is *that* what this is all about?"

Reese shook his head. "No, this is about revenge. I came back here…to hurt you."

Eliza's back went stiff. Her eyes filled with moisture. "I know," she said, then added softly, "you succeeded."

Reese took a long pull of oxygen. "I'm used to getting what I want, Eliza. And I wanted you to see my success. To see what you missed out on. I wanted to make you sorry for walking out on me."

"I've been sorry," she said, her voice not much more than a squeak, then added quietly, "but you've been… cruel." She rose from her seat, her stance firm, and spoke without hesitation. "I want those divorce papers now, Reese. The game is over."

Reese shook his head and said calmly, "Sit down, Eliza."

"Why? Why should I let you—"

"You wanted the truth and I gave it to you. This isn't a game."

She scoffed, her eyes going bright with indignation, "No, this is a divorce."

"Is that what you really want—a divorce?" he asked, uncertain of her answer. He'd give her the damn divorce if she really wanted it. But he wasn't going to let her waltz out of his life again.

Eliza blinked, appearing deep in thought, then slowly lowered herself to her chair. When she looked at him, her eyes beseeched his. "Is that what *you* really want?"

A slow, sexy ballad played softly in the background, the band forgoing the lyrics to simply let the music tell the story. Reese rose and took her hand. "What I want is to dance with my wife."

Eliza's eyes blazed. "And Reese always gets what he wants?"

"I don't know…you tell me," he said, changing course and smiling down at her, stroking his thumb over her hand gently. "Will you dance with me?"

"It's not two-stepping music," she said cautiously, her resolve and anger ebbing. He felt the release of tension under his palm.

"You should know by now—I'm not a two-stepping kind of man."

Eliza stared into his eyes, watching him closely as if making up her mind.

"Come on. I want to hold you in my arms." Reese tugged her hand and she rose willingly.

He guided her onto the dance floor and wrapped his arms around her, bringing her close enough to share body heat. "You smell good, Eliza." He nuzzled her throat, breathing more of her in, then tightened his hold on her. "Feel good in my arms."

She resisted for a second, then set her head on his shoulder and they swayed slightly back and forth to the rhythm of the music. "I'm not going to sleep with you tonight," she announced quietly.

Reese had to smile. "I know. I want to take you out again tomorrow night."

Eliza sighed into his chest and waited half a beat before answering. "Okay."

Not sleeping with Reese last night had taken its toll on Eliza. She'd been angry and hurt with him and his brutal truths. But afterward, he'd been respectful of her wishes, understanding her gentle fury at his deception. He'd been a perfect gentleman, taking her home, planting a quick, chaste good-night kiss on her lips at her door before driving off.

For some odd reason, Eliza felt she'd won a round with him. And she'd realized that Reese had been right in clearing the air between them. She wanted honesty.

She got honesty.

But tonight was different. She couldn't wait to see him. She couldn't wait to see what the promise of a night free of lies and deception would bring.

She'd thought about him all night. And this morning, while at the Children's Center committee meeting, she'd been told that an anonymous donor had pledged an obscene amount of money for a new children's playground in Sioux Falls. The donor refused any recognition whatsoever. But Eliza knew. It had to be Reese. Money didn't drop out of the blue like that. In all her years in fund-raising, she'd never had someone donate without being given their due credit. Corporations wanted the good press a hefty donation would bring; private donors liked having their names associated with the project.

But just to be sure, she'd pried the information out of the treasurer, a good friend who owed her a big favor.

Eliza hadn't been shocked when she'd seen the name on the pledge sheet. She'd been…humbled.

And so pleased she could hardly keep from jumping his bones when he picked her up looking gorgeous dressed in a black tuxedo.

As they entered the elevator to his penthouse, Eliza felt his eyes on her, watching her every move with a hot gleam. She felt daring tonight, donning her new Ralph Lauren cream halter dress, scooped low in front, decorated with enough gold sequins to make King Tut jealous. The only jewelry she wore was long, delicate chandelier earrings that nearly touched her shoulders.

Reese had taken off her coat in the lobby of the hotel and raked her over with a dangerous look that had sent hot shivers down to her gold-mesh-sandal-encased toes and back.

"You trying to kill me, darlin'?" he asked, eyeing her breasts that nearly scooped out of the scoop neck.

Eliza smiled coyly, glad they were alone in the elevator. "Only a little."

Reese raised a brow. "As long as we're being honest," he said, moving closer and taking her in his arms, "I've always wanted to do this." He lifted her chin with one finger, while the fingers of his other hand wreaked havoc on her cleavage. He lowered his head, brushing his lips to her mouth first, then nibbled lower, down her chin, her throat, until he cut a moist, hot path to her breasts. He fondled one, dipping his hand inside the stretchy material, rocking Eliza back on her heels and against the elevator wall, while his mouth devoured the other, just above the cut of the very low, sweeping neckline.

She rested her head back, giving him full access and breathed out, "You've never done this?"

"Not in an elevator. Not with you," he said between kisses. When the elevator stopped on the fifteenth floor, he groaned, then righted the material on her dress, kissed her quickly and took her hand.

They exited the elevator and walked only a short distance to the penthouse's double-door entrance. Before allowing her inside, he moved her against the door, pressing his body to hers and trapping her with two hands braced on the door. "Here's the deal. If you say no to me tonight, I'll respect that, but you'll be contributing to my slow and painful demise."

When he kissed her, his mouth competed with his granite-hard erection for her attention. It was quite a contest, one she enjoyed completely. He'd made his point and Eliza relished the heady sensation of being given a choice. Reese didn't demand and she liked seeing him with his guard down for a change.

He smiled at her, that dimple peeking out again, heating her blood, and Eliza figured she'd have to be made of stone to deny him anything tonight.

Reese was sure she'd worn that dress to torture him. She was succeeding. Conservative, demure Eliza, went for bold and sexy tonight. With candlelight flickering across the room, she stood facing him, eyeing the elegantly dressed table set for two. The soft light cast her in a golden glow, complementing the highlights in her upswept hair, the rosy hue on her face, the long, slender cut of that dress and legs that brought his view down to sexy, gilded mile-high heels.

He envisioned her wearing nothing *but* those heels, all tall, tan and temptingly naked. Reese wanted her again. Bad. But he wanted something more from her.

Her trust.

Even now, as her gaze roamed the penthouse suite, taking in crystal vases of tulips and tapered candles glowing, with soft music playing, he noted wariness in her eyes. Her mind seemed to be clicking away, wondering if she could place her faith in him.

He couldn't blame her. He'd set out to hurt her and he had. But his plan had backfired. He couldn't walk away from her as he'd intended.

Lucky for him, he'd recognized what was most important to him, revenge being the furthest thing from his mind. Now he planned on helping Eliza heal from wounds he'd inflicted and from older, deeper wounds he'd had no part in exacting.

He wanted to be alone with her tonight, yet he'd intended on taking it slowly. He'd planned on keeping his hands off. He'd planned on enjoying time with her innocently. That's what second dates should be all about—learning about each other, gaining a certain attainable trust. Not rushing things.

Until he'd gotten a look at her in those clothes.

Reese was no fool. She'd dressed for seduction tonight.

Who was he to deny her?

"Are you hungry?" he asked, glancing down at the dome lids covering a savory meal.

Eliza tilted her head to one side and approached him. "That depends."

"On?"

"What you're serving." Her scent wafted in the air, fresh and exotic all at the same time.

Reese popped the champagne cork, keeping his gaze fastened on her. He poured two flutes and handed her one, their fingers brushing from the slight contact. "Champagne for now. Anything you want for later."

"Mmm," she said, sipping her drink and sliding her eyes closed, the look on her face so damn sensual that Reese's blood pressure shot up. "Sounds…good."

Reese narrowed his eyes. "You're a tease, Eliza."

Slowly she opened her eyes. "You liked that about me once."

He sipped his champagne. "I *love* that about you now."

The flute in her hand visibly shook. She lowered the glass down and stared at him, searching for the truth. "I can't do this again, Reese. Not unless you're serious."

Reese set his champagne glass down. "I told you once—this isn't a game. I'm serious."

Eliza bit down on her lower lip, then shook her bangs from her eyes. "So we're seriously dating?"

Reese grinned. "You're putting a label on something that doesn't need one, darlin'."

"*I* need one."

"Okay," he said, picking up the flute again. "Let's drink to seriously dating each other."

Eliza lifted her flute and, with a soft clink, sealed the deal.

"Now that we've settled that, do you want to sit down and have dinner?" he asked.

"As opposed to?"

Reese undid his tie, removed his tux jacket, tossing them both on the wing chair beside the sofa as he gazed at her with heat smoldering in his eyes. He undid all the buttons on his shirt, letting the shirt hang against bronzed skin and a hard body. He took her hand, planted a kiss on her palm, then slid it down to his belt buckle, flattening her fingers to his painful erection. He shot her a daring look. "Making love by the skyline, destroying the sheets on my bed, steaming up the hot tub."

She batted her eyes and smiled seductively. "All of the above?"

He smiled. "Done."

Nine

Reese led Eliza over to the elegant sliding doors that looked out to a balcony. Stars twinkled overhead, challenging the city lights for brilliance. Between the two, the sky sparkled like diamonds.

"It's a good night to be inside, looking out," Reese said, standing behind her. He nuzzled her neck with his nose, then planted hot, moist kisses there. Eliza's breath caught in her throat. "It's a good night to be inside…*you*."

Every night was a good night for that, she thought wickedly.

Reese untied the straps of her halter, exposing her shoulders. He kissed the nape of her neck again, then moved on to the bared skin of her collarbone. Slowly he slid the straps farther down until the material was held up solely by the round curves of her breasts. With a gentle tug, Reese pulled her free of the rest of the dress. It slid down her body smoothly and heaped into a puddle of gold sequins.

Reese cupped her breasts from behind, his hands firm and possessive as he flicked her nipples with his thumbs. Eliza slid her eyes closed and rested her head back against his chest. "Reese," she said breathlessly, "we're in front of the window."

And she was naked but for her heels and lacy thong.

"No one can see us way up here, darlin'. Enjoy the view," he said, then spun her around to stare into her eyes. "I know I am."

His mouth came down on hers, devouring her with hot, lusty strokes of his tongue and softly murmured commands. He spun her around again, bringing her fully up against him, and held her tight, with one hand gripping her hips, the other threading underneath her thong and sinking into her soft feminine curls.

"Oh." She slid her eyes closed again and moaned from the intense pleasure Reese created with his fingers. Behind her, he was rock-hard, rubbing into her and reminding her of the fulfillment yet to come.

He stroked her with finesse, finding all the right places. She swayed her body, unable to control the rocking sensations hitting her full force.

He kissed her throat and whispered in her ear, "I'm gonna watch you explode, darlin'." She popped her eyes open, seeing him in the reflection of the glass-paned sliding doors.

Seeing them both in the reflection, the erotic picture

they made and Reese's intense look, she'd never been more aroused. Exposed in front of the door, she knew that no one could see her through the darkness and height and yet she'd never felt so completely free.

Eliza lifted both arms up above her head to work her fingers through his hair, holding on tight, her breaths coming harder now. She made little throaty sounds, and Reese encouraged her with sexy, erotic words. "You're almost there, baby. You're so damn beautiful when you co—"

"Reese, Reese," she moaned as blasting heat and electric tingles racked her body. She swayed, she moved, she stilled. And the explosion shook her, consuming her, the release leaving her with a heady thrill of completion.

Reese held her from behind, letting her come down slowly, kissing her throat, patiently waiting.

She turned in his arms. She still wanted him. She wanted more. She pulsed with the need to have him fill her. "Let's go destroy your sheets," she whispered.

"That's my girl." Reese lifted her up and carried her to the bedroom.

Eliza smiled thinking that there was no doubt about it. She *was* Reese Parker's girl.

Reese laid her down on his bed, looking at the perfect picture she made there with tousled hair fanning out, bared to him but for the creamy lace thong and those killer heels. It was where she belonged—in his bed, with him, forever. He'd come to that realization some time ago but refused to allow the thought to become reality. He'd been blinded by his need for payback, retribution, revenge. But now he'd seen her in her element, seeing the real Eliza for the first time. She wasn't just the bold, sexy woman he'd met one summer day in Montana. No, she was vulnerable and sensitive and compassionate. Extremely intelligent and competent. Caring. She had talent that she was afraid to pursue, dreams she put on hold. She wanted what most people wanted—to be loved fully and completely.

Reese had given her that kind of love before and it had gone bad. But he was willing to try again, willing to put the past behind him.

He'd fallen in love with her again.

He watched her wiggle out of her thong, gliding it down her body.

"Don't you dare take off those heels."

A low rumbling chuckle came out of her throat. "You mean these?" She lifted one leg, pointing her toes at him.

"Yes, damn it."

He cast off his shirt quickly and reached for his belt buckle, but Eliza covered his hand with hers. "Let me."

Reese dropped his hands to his side.

She rose up on her knees, unfastened his belt, unzipped his pants and reached in, taking him into her hands. Reese slammed his eyes shut, his hands going into her hair, threading through as she stroked him tenderly. When she shifted gears, taking him into her mouth, he flinched—the hot, moist pressure nearly doing him in. After a minute of intense pleasure, Reese stopped her. "Enough."

Eliza understood. They knew each other so well. She lay back down, her eyes fastened on him.

He shed the rest of his clothes and covered her

with his body, spreading her legs and finding her wet heat. He thrust inside her, claiming her with powerful, potent, overwhelming need. He moved. She moved. They rocked together, the heels of those sandals scraping his back.

It happened fast from then on, hurried, wild. Reese poured everything he had into her until both met with a fierce overwhelming climax.

He came down to kiss her again and again. She kissed him back just as readily and something changed between them then. Something strong and urgent. And he sensed the moment when Eliza found her trust in him.

She smiled, her eyes filled with a soft glow.

Reese took hold of her hand and kissed it, then locked their fingers together. He'd forgotten to use protection. It had happened so fast, the need so urgent. Or had it been a deliberate act? Had he purposely shoved those thoughts away? Reese had always wanted children with Eliza.

They still had issues. Eliza was lying to her family about him. She'd been omitting the truth for six years. He'd leave it up to her how to resolve that problem.

He was due back in Montana tomorrow. He had a business to run. There'd been a small fire at one of the oil wells. Luckily it had been contained before it had spread, but two of his crew had been injured. He'd just learned of it this afternoon and needed to find out the details. Breaking this date with Eliza hadn't been an option. They were on fragile ground here, and he'd set out to earn her trust and heal past wounds. She was too important to him now. But Reese had to return to

Bozeman. He owed those injured workers a visit and he needed to see a report on the fire.

He rolled on his side, resting on his elbow to look at her. She had her eyes closed, a look of sated tranquility on her face. She caught him watching her and smiled. "What?"

"You look…happy."

She bit her lower lip and nodded. "I am." Then she rolled on her side and her beautiful full breasts jiggled from the movement. "Are you?"

Reese nearly snorted. "I'm in bed with a gorgeous woman, about to make love to her again. Oh…I'm happy."

Eliza rode her fingers across his chest. "Again?"

"Or we can have dinner now? Hot tub? Whatever you want. Reese Parker aims to please."

She giggled. "Oh, you're pleasing me."

Reese took her into his arms, curling her body into his. He breathed in her scent, that exotic mix of female smells that drove him crazy. "Stay with me tonight. I want to wake up with you in my arms."

Eliza hesitated a moment, and Reese realized she was planning her next lie to her family. She was a grown woman with a life of her own, but she lived in the family home. They'd know that she'd stayed out all night. There would probably be questions. Reese read all that in the tentative look on her face.

She sighed heavily and closed her eyes, then reopened them with a steady look. "I'll stay the night."

The next morning Eliza heard the steady hum of water running in the shower and then a squeak in the plumbing when the faucet was turned off. She opened her eyes and watched Reese as he entered the bedroom. Smelling clean, his hair tousled and still damp from his shower, she followed his fluid movements as he dressed into a pair of dark slacks and a fresh white shirt. His gaze met hers as he buttoned up his shirt. "Stay in bed. Sleep. It's early and I kept you up late last night."

Eliza smiled warmly, vivid memories flooding in as to exactly how Reese had kept her up last night. She stretched, her arms going up over her head, and the sheet dropped down a bit, uncovering her nude body.

Reese groaned, sat down on the bed and kissed her gently on the lips as he covered her up again. "Don't tempt me. I have an early flight out." He set the key card on the dresser next to her. "Stay as long as you like. I'll be back Friday night."

As much as Reese's tone indicated he'd rather be in bed with her, his expression was all business. He'd already dismissed her, his mind focused on his company and what he had to do this week. It was crazy, but she missed him already. She glanced at the key card he trusted her with and felt that they were finally making progress. "I'll see you Friday night, then?"

He nodded. "For our third date."

She grinned. "It'd be kind of hard to top last night."

Reese reached out and twirled a strand of her hair around his fingers. "If you don't mind being seen around town with me, I'll be sure to make our next date just as memorable."

Eliza sighed, then took a big swallow, reminded of all the lies she'd told her family about her relationship with Reese. If she and Reese were seen around town together, the news would get back to them. The family would know that they were dating, and even though her father had alluded to it, she'd denied anything was going on again and again. Eliza knew her days and lies were numbered. She wanted to tell her family the truth. If only she could bring herself to do it. But her father had been distracted lately and Patricia had never seemed more unapproachable. The thought of owning up to her secret six-year marriage weighed heavily on her.

"Reese, I need a little more time," she said softly.

He gazed deep into her eyes. "I came back for you, Eliza."

"I…know." And she was glad of it now.

"No, you don't understand. Six years ago. I came here to see you after you walked out on me."

"What?" Eliza lifted the covers nearly to her chin and bolted up in bed. "When?"

"A few days after getting your note. You burned me bad and I was pissed and hurt and confused. I stewed on it and once I'd calmed a little, I knew that I couldn't let you just walk out of my life so easily. So I came here looking for…I don't know. A fight, I guess. Something. I had to know what happened."

"What did happen? I…we…never saw each other."

"Your brother Case tossed me off your property. Wouldn't let me in the house."

Stunned, Eliza could barely make sense of this. "Why not?"

Reese snorted, then laughed wryly. "He didn't want a drunken cowboy anywhere near his sister. She'd had enough of a bad time lately, he said and then threatened to call the police." Reese continued to twirl her hair, watching it twine around his finger rather than witness the pained expression on her face.

"I'm sorry. If Case had known who you were… maybe—"

"He was protecting his sister. I got that. But even then, I didn't reveal your secret. I've waited six years, darlin'. I suppose I can wait a little longer for you."

Eliza never loved Reese more than at that moment. No longer demanding and imposing, he'd opened up his heart and quietly given her the time she needed. "Thank you for coming after me," she said, her eyes filling with tears, thinking if Case had only allowed Reese entrance to her home the last six years might have been spent differently. But that was water under the bridge and she wouldn't dwell on the past. Still, it gladdened her heart that he had cared enough to come after her and confirmed that she wasn't making another mistake with Reese. "And thank you for giving me the time I need now."

He tugged her hair, letting it go completely, then brushed a sweet kiss across her mouth. "Friday night."

Eliza lingered in his bed long after he'd gone. Sated from a night of lovemaking and thrilled to have Reese back in her life, especially now that he'd confessed to coming after her, she'd never felt more certain about him. Or more content.

As tentative as their relationship was right now, Eliza knew that they were headed on the right path. And it no longer frightened her. She'd given up on her mistrust of Reese, letting down the barriers that had kept them apart.

She stayed in his penthouse suite most of the morning, showering and dressing lazily, then she called a taxi. During the ride home, she decided on telling her father that she was dating Reese Parker. If questioned further, she'd own up to spending the night with him last night, as if Nash wouldn't have already assumed that from seeing her return home in evening clothes.

With bravado, Eliza entered her home, fully prepared to shed some minor truths regarding her relationship with Reese. However, she found the house empty but for Ivy, who was preparing tonight's dinner, and Peggy, who was busy polishing silver in the dining room.

"Hi, Peg," she said, taking a seat in the dining room with elbows braced on the table and hands holding up her chin, just as she had as a little girl. Eliza had always loved to watch Peggy's regimented process of shining up the silver.

"Morning, Eliza." Then with a raised eyebrow she said, "Or should I say good afternoon, dear girl."

Eliza laughed.

"I see you've got a few wrinkles on your dress," she said lightly. "I'll have it dry-cleaned for you."

Eliza blushed. "Thanks."

"I like seeing the smile in your eyes. It's been too long."

"Are my eyes smiling now?" she asked Peggy, remembering that she'd say that very thing whenever Eliza was extremely happy.

"As bright as when you found the most Easter eggs during the hunt or when your father surprised you with your first car. Or the day you showed me your Wellesley diploma."

Eliza shrugged. "I guess...I'm happy."

Peggy wiped the knife clean of polish, stroking the blade back and forth with a soft cloth as Eliza looked on. "That Reese Parker is a nice man."

This time Eliza wouldn't argue. Eliza felt it deep down in her bones. "Yes, I think so, too."

Peggy shot her a knowing glance. "Next time maybe you'll think to bring a change of clothes."

"*Thinking* didn't have much to do with it, Peg."

This time Peggy blushed, turning the aging housekeeper's face rosy red. "Ah, that man is lucky to have you, Eliza. I hope he realizes that."

"Yes, I hope so, too," she said, wondering if she and Reese had a real chance at happiness the second time around.

Ten

Reese sat in the wingback chair in his penthouse suite, going over ground surveys for three new drilling sites with Leanne. She sat on the sofa with papers, reports and financial statements spread out on the marble cocktail table. Leanne's dark eyeglasses kept slipping down and she kept setting them in place with the slightest touch of her finger.

Reese chuckled and she lifted her eyes.

"You're a good sport for agreeing to this," he said.

"I've never been to Sioux Falls before. Not that I've seen much of the town since we landed this morning."

"I've kept you pretty busy, I know. But it's important to me, Leanne. I need to be here right now."

She nodded, eying him with a question on her lips, but luckily she thought better of it. Reese appreciated that. He'd kept his marriage and his life private for a long time. Now wasn't the time to open up to her or anyone else, for that matter. Not until his relationship with Eliza was resolved.

He'd gone back to Montana for two days and decided enough was enough. He wanted to see Eliza tonight, a full twenty-four hours sooner than she expected him. He'd called her every day since leaving her in this suite the other morning, but had been too tied up with work to spend any real time on the phone with her. Then he'd decided the hell with it. He was the boss. If he wanted to be in Sioux Falls with Eliza, he'd just bring his work along with him.

And his associate, Leanne Finnegan.

An hour later, Leanne lifted her head, tilting it from side to side, then rubbed the tension out of her neck.

Reese watched her, noting how pretty she was. Beautiful, really, and probably the perfect match for his brother.

He tossed his papers down. "Quitting time," he said. "And not a moment too soon, I see. Are your eyes crossing yet?"

Leanne grinned. "I'll live, Reese."

"God, I hope so."

Leanne set her own survey reports down on the cocktail table and, sitting up straight in her seat, she took off her glasses. Then, in an efficient move, she removed the pins from her hair, and dark, silky waves poured over her shoulders. "Mind if I ask you something?" she said quietly, scooting her way along the sofa to get closer to him.

Reese leaned back in his chair. "Not at all. What's on your mind?"

Leanne took a deep breath. "Do you think I'm attractive?"

Surprised, Reese hid his stunned expression and kept his voice even. "I'd say you're beautiful, Leanne. Why?"

She seemed edgier than he'd ever seen her. She bit her lip, and when she sighed, Reese noted the rise and fall of her breasts. Even though she wore a no-nonsense pin-striped business suit, any man with eyes in his head would know that she had a gorgeous body.

She kept her dark eyes fastened to his. "What if I told you I'm attracted to someone I work with?"

"Uh, well…that would be okay," he said, his nerves jumbling a bit and wariness creeping in. "As long as it didn't interfere with your performance…at work, I mean." Suddenly he felt like Dr. Phil. And he certainly didn't like the way she was staring at him as though he could make or break her with his replies.

"So you wouldn't think it unprofessional? Because I'd have to make the first move. He doesn't seem to know I exist."

He watched her move even closer to him, her eyes vivid, clear and intense. Reese rubbed his temple, keeping his panic down. Hell, if Leanne was interested in him, he'd missed all the signs. Heaven help him, he'd never want to hurt her. Or lose her. She was the best geologist in the business. Had he given her the wrong idea, asking her to join him here in Sioux Falls? "Leanne, you're not giving yourself enough credit. Any man would know—"

She touched his arm, stopping his next thought. "Not just any man, Reese."

Reese froze. Her fingers slid across his shirt.

"Your brother."

His dread evaporated instantly and he was filled with astounding relief. The irony almost killing him, he barely contained his composure. "Garrett?"

She nodded. "Is he seeing someone?"

Only you, in his dreams, Reese almost blurted out.

"No, he's not seeing anyone. In fact, Leanne, I'd say this is a great time to let him know how you feel."

"Really? And it would be okay with you?"

Reese smiled. "More than okay with me." He winked. "Don't worry. Somehow I think Garrett won't mind one bit."

Leanne sank back on the sofa looking more than mildly relieved. "Thank you, Reese. You won't say anything, right?"

"My lips are sealed," he said, thinking that Garrett was one lucky son of a gun, to have the woman of his dreams make a play for him without any secrets, lies or deception. Reese was elated to be off the hook, and now his brother would come to know some happiness in his life. Hell, he'd been pining away for Leanne for months now, too damn intimated by his own feelings to make a move. "Come on, let's get this work together. Then we'll grab a quick dinner."

"Sounds good to me," she said, gathering up all the papers she'd brought and setting them inside her briefcase. With a click of the case, she turned to add, "All ready. I'm starving. Do you know where we can get some good hometown cooking?"

"Actually, I know this little honky-tonk." Reese

helped her on with her coat and they smiled at each other before he put a hand to her back and guided her to the door.

Reese reached for the knob just as the door opened from the other side with a decided click.

Eliza stood on the threshold.

With wide assessing eyes, she stood ramrod still for one moment, her gaze darting from him to Leanne and back, taking in his hand on Leanne's back and the smiles on their faces. Eliza's mouth dropped open. There was no mistaking her thoughts. Everything was revealed to him, from the pained look on her face to the hot, angry tears welling in her eyes.

She stepped back just as he reached out to her. "Eliza, wait…"

She shook her head and kept backing away. "Don't, Reese. Just don't. I get it now," she said, with near hysterical laughter.

"Damn it, Eliza. This isn't what it—"

"I've been such a fool," she declared, "and now your revenge is finally complete!"

Before he had a second to formulate just the right words, she turned on her heel and ran straight to the elevator, climbing in. The door slid closed before Reese had a chance to catch her, but in that one instant he noted heated accusation in her eyes and sheer devastation on her face.

Reese leaned heavily on the doorjamb and closed his eyes. Eliza could have waited for his explanation. She could have heard him out. Instead, she chose to believe the worst about him. She didn't trust him. She never had. And he feared that maybe she never would. Sadly Reese also realized that Eliza had no faith in herself or what they meant to each other.

Leanne touched his arm. "Reese, I'm so sorry. Did I do—"

He shook his head and cast her a solemn look. "It's not your fault, Leanne. Mistakes were made a long time ago. And now we're both paying the price."

"I didn't know you were involved with anyone, Reese. By the look on your face, I'd say it was pretty serious."

"*Intense* is the correct word."

"Who is she?" Leanne asked, then waved off the question. "Never mind. It's not my business."

Reese sighed heavily. Hell, Leanne had confided in him about Garrett, so why not confide in her about Eliza? Right now, with his heart heavy, he could use a friend. "She's my...wife."

The only woman I've ever loved.

Eliza drove home frenzied, the pain almost unbearable. She parked the car outside the front door of her home and hurried inside, bumping into Patricia and her father in the foyer.

"Eliza, what's wrong?" Patricia asked, a deep frown on her face. This was one time Eliza didn't need or want Patricia's concern. At any other time she would have relished it, but now she just wanted to be left alone.

"Nothing," she said, lying once again. "I'm not feeling well." She bypassed her father and headed for the staircase.

"Eliza," her father called out.

"I'll...be...fine, Dad," she said, climbing the stairs quickly, heading to her room. She slammed her bedroom door and then leaned heavily against it, relieved to finally be alone, away from more lies, hurt and deception.

Her tears fell rapidly, freely, streaming down her face. She wouldn't have to pretend to anyone that everything was all right. Here, in the sanctity of her bedroom, she could cry her eyes out and let her heart bleed for a love that shouldn't have ever happened. She sank down to the floor, confused, hurt and angry.

Reese couldn't have planned it any better, could he? He'd led her to believe he was sincere, wanting a fresh start, and she'd fallen for it and him—again. Seeing him with another woman, one who'd made him smile, one who had looked at him with such blatant admiration, had nearly destroyed her. Had he been in Sioux Falls all along? Maybe he hadn't left that morning, at all. Maybe he'd planned on duping her longer, but her showing up unexpectedly certainly couldn't have been planned. She asked herself once again, what kind of game was Reese playing?

Her cell phone rang.

Eliza wouldn't look at the number on the screen.

She couldn't talk to anyone right now.

She lifted it out of her purse and shut it off.

Then she dug into her purse again, pulling out the envelope and the note she'd written to Reese, the note she couldn't wait to have him read, the reason she'd gone to his penthouse this evening in the first place.

Through a waterfall of tears, she skimmed the writing with disgust.

Dear Reese,

I've finally realized that the lying and deception must stop. It's not fair to you or to me. By the time you read this, I will have told my family the truth about our marriage and the lies I've told for six years. I can only hope they will understand when I apologize. I love you, Reese. I always have. We both deserve to have our marriage out in the open, free of secrets. I will see you soon and hopefully we can put the past behind us once and for all.

Your wife,
Eliza

Eliza ripped up the note and tossed it away, but the sad ache in her belly remained. She'd never known such pain.

She lay down on her bed, rehashing the time she'd spent with Reese, looking for clues, trying to figure out why she hadn't seen this coming. Was she that big a fool?

Reese hadn't looked guilty when she'd found him with another woman. He'd only looked surprised. She'd caught him red-handed. Or had she?

For the first time in her life, Eliza really reexamined what she'd seen, both six years ago in that hotel room and tonight. Could Reese possibly have been innocent? On both accounts? Had she walked in on something tonight that could easily be explained?

Eliza shoved her eyes closed, the turmoil of the past few weeks taking a heavy toll on her body and her mind. She needed to rest, to clear her head.

She couldn't think anymore.

She slept until a soft knocking on her door roused her. "Eliza, it's me, Nicole."

"Nic?" Drowsy and disoriented, Eliza sat up in bed. "What are you doing here?" Once the events of the past few hours rushed in, Eliza regained some composure. She realized the time. She hadn't slept all night but only a few hours. She got up and opened the door.

Nic stood in the doorway holding a big Louis Vuitton bag. "Your dad called me. He's worried about you."

"Oh," she said, moving aside to let her friend in. "That's not like him."

"Well, forgive me, but you look like hell. I can understand why he'd worry. What happened?"

Eliza sat down on her bed and Nic followed. "*Reese* happened." Then she glanced at her bag. "What'd you bring?"

Nic smiled. "Pajama party." She lifted out two pairs of pajamas decorated with red cherries and green stems, a bottle of wine and two crystal glasses.

Eliza's mood lightened temporarily. Through their teen years, they'd always managed to console each other with a sleepover and lots of good honest talk. The wine came as an added feature in their adulthood. "How'd you know?"

Nic took hold of her hand. "Like you said, Reese happened. We'll get in our pajamas later. Right now let's have a glass of wine and talk, okay?"

Eliza nodded. Nicole was the only person she trusted with her thoughts, doubts, fears and mistakes. "You pour the wine. I'll pour out my heart."

"That bad?" Nicole asked, a look of deep concern on her face.

"Nic, I'm either the biggest fool in the world or I've made another huge mistake in judgment. Maybe both."

Nicole opened the bottle of wine and poured two glasses, handing her one. "I'm listening."

Eliza began, "Well, I don't how it could get much worse...."

"This isn't the worst thing in the world, Nash."

Eliza woke to the sound of her stepmother's elevated voice coming from right outside her bedroom door. She opened her eyes, squinting at the daylight pouring inside her window. Glancing at the clock, she realized the late morning hour. She'd overslept.

"Give her a chance to explain," she heard Patricia say.

"She lied to all of us," Nash said to his wife. "You know how I feel about liars. Eliza, wake up."

Her father's stern voice jarred her into action. She sat up in bed, rubbing her forehead and the fuzziness away. She and Nicole had overindulged a little last night, the numbing power of a great Chardonnay finally ebbing.

"We've been waiting for you to get up for an hour," her father called out from outside her door.

Eliza's brows furrowed in confusion when she saw the *Tribune* newspaper sliding under her door.

"Get dressed, Eliza. And come downstairs. You have some explaining to do."

She hadn't heard that tone from her father since, as a young girl, she'd taken a feisty mare out for a ride

without permission. The horse had tossed her off as she
rounded the corner of the stables, right in front of her
father's eyes.

"I'll be down, Dad. Give me a minute." She rose immediately and picked up the newspaper left under her
door, the headlines glaring and unmistakable no matter
how many times she blinked her eyes. "Oh, no!"

*Fortune Heiress's Summer Fling and Secret Mar-
riage Revealed!*

Eliza's heart slammed against her chest.

She continued to read the words that burned a hole
in the pit of her stomach.

> *Eliza Fortune, chairperson and benefactor to
> many South Dakota charity organizations, hid her
> secret six-year Montana marriage to former rodeo
> champion Reese Parker from family and friends.
> Apparently her wild summer fling ended badly, and
> now Mrs. Reese Parker is being sued for divorce.*

Eliza finished reading the article that portrayed her
as a fickle, insecure, spoiled woman who rebounded
after her broken engagement with mayoral candidate
Warren Keyes, duping both her family and close friends
by hiding her marriage to a onetime down-on-his-luck
rodeo rider. The article went on to describe Reese as a
prosperous oilman who'd made his way up the ranks
despite his estranged marriage to the Fortune heiress,
wanting out of the union at any cost.

Eliza's head throbbed. She'd never meant to hurt her
family. She'd decided to tell them the truth despite what

had happened last night with Reese. But someone had beaten her to it. And she suspected she knew who'd leaked this story to the press.

Trina Watters, Nash's ex-wife and her half-brother Blake's, biological mother. The woman had been accused of causing trouble for both Case and Gina and Max and Diana. A bitter woman, she seemed to find some sort of delight and satisfaction at hurting Nash and his family.

Eliza finger-combed her hair, changed into a pair of black slacks and a warm beige cashmere sweater, set her feet into suede loafers and went downstairs. During the night, after a good long, revealing talk with Nicole, she'd come to some important decisions that would affect her entire life.

Today she planned on making things right and finally, once and for all, taking charge of her life.

Her bravado faded somewhat when she entered the great room to find Case, Creed and her father staring at her from their allotted seats around the room as though she'd stolen the Hope diamond.

The only friendly face was Patricia's. Eliza appreciated her support, even if she had been remote lately. "Good morning."

Male voices grumbled their greeting.

"Sit down, Eliza," Patricia said with kindness. "I've poured you a cup of coffee. Ivy set out some pastries. Would you care for one?"

Eliza sat down to face her family, with Patricia seated next to Nash on the sofa and her brothers in wingback chairs on either side of them. "No, thanks, Patricia. I'm not…" She glanced at her father's expectant face, then at her two older brothers. "I don't have an appetite."

The room was quiet, and Eliza knew she had an audience and her family's full attention. "I'm sorry for all this. Truly. I can't tell you how much I hated lying to all of you. I hope you can forgive me, but most of what the article said is true. I left here six years ago after finding Warren in bed with his campaign manager. It was a hard time in my life. I went to Montana to escape the scrutiny and all the press. You all know the reasons I didn't reveal the truth about Warren to the press. I was trying to protect the family and our good name. Trying not to cause a scandal. A broken engagement is surely less seedy than the real reason I walked out on him.

"When I went to Montana, the last thing I expected was to start another relationship. But I did. I fell deeply in love with a kind, sweet-natured rodeo rider. Reese. I realized then what love really was—at least I thought I did. Reese and I had a wonderful summer together. We married quickly."

Nash's intake of breath resounded in the quiet room.

Eliza's expression implored her father. "I'm sorry I didn't tell you. I wanted…some time. Some privacy. And then, shortly after, my marriage to Reese fell apart."

"What happened, Eliza?" her father asked.

"It was a big misunderstanding. I jumped to wrong conclusions. I guess I'd still been smarting from Warren's betrayal. But I didn't realize it at that time. I walked out on Reese and came home."

"You couldn't have loved him much," Case said pointedly.

Eliza shook her head. "Oh, quite the opposite, big brother. It killed me to walk out on him. We'd been so happy. I came home feeling like a failure. Twice I'd been hurt. Twice I felt I'd been betrayed. I didn't want another scandal. I realized how the press would spin the story. I worried about our family's reputation and…my own. My charity work would have suffered. But I'd been wrong about Reese. Yes, he came here for a divorce. But since we've spent time together, I realized that I still love him with my whole heart. And if he'll take me back, I want our marriage to work."

"Why wouldn't he take you back? He certainly hasn't been acting like a man with divorce on his mind," Nash said.

Eliza wrinkled her nose and decided to keep the details of her last encounter with Reese private and the fact that he'd come here initially with revenge on his mind. "Uh, well, there might have been another misunderstanding. But I've learned my lesson. I'm not about to let go of the man I love. Not this time."

Eliza glanced at her brothers, who seemed to have eased the tight expressions on their faces. Then she glanced at Patricia. She nodded in understanding, her eyes soft and beckoning Nash to do the same.

"If you'd have told us the truth six years ago, we would have worked it all out as a family," her father said quietly.

Patricia spoke up. "Eliza thought she was protecting us."

"Plus, I felt so humiliated, Dad. I couldn't put our family through another one of my messes, just months after my broken engagement."

Nash nodded. "I can understand that, honey." Then he took Patricia's hand. "I wish you hadn't lied to us, but I forgive you."

Patricia stiffened visibly but cast her a soft smile. "There's nothing to forgive. You only did what you thought was right."

Eliza let out a heavy sigh, relieved that her secret was finally out in the open. "Thank you—all of you—for listening. And not judging me."

"We love you, Eliza," her father said, "and want you to be happy. I like Reese."

"You do?"

"He's a self-made man. And he married my daughter."

"But someone's out to hurt our family, Dad. Leaking that story to the *Tribune* smells of Trina's handiwork," Case said with an angry gleam in his eyes.

"I think it was her, too, Dad. I'm going to talk to Blake and see if he can do something about her." Eliza finally sipped her coffee, her stomach unclenching now. Though the thought of accusing Blake's mother wasn't a welcome one, Eliza had always been able to talk to him. Unlike her brothers, who never gave Blake a chance.

Creed snorted. "Blake has no control over her."

"You aren't being fair to him," Eliza said. "Neither one of you has ever given him the benefit of the doubt."

Case and Creed remained silent.

"He's over at Skylar's now. See if you can talk some sense into him," her father said.

"I'm going to, Dad. And thank you for understanding about me and Reese."

Nash rose and walked over to her. He took her hand and she lifted her face up to meet his smile. "You have my blessing, honey. Patricia and I only want you to be happy."

Eliza glanced at Patricia, who also smiled. Something was going on between her father and Patricia, but Eliza couldn't quite put her finger on it. Yet she relished her family's forgiveness and made a promise to herself to do her best to make things right between her and Reese.

Nic had really helped her realize one very important thing last night: Eliza had never fought for her marriage. She'd never stuck around long enough to listen to Reese and hear his explanations. She'd readily made wrong assumptions about him and their marriage. Five un-answered cell phone calls from Reese last night had her believing in him again. He'd cared. He'd called. He'd wanted to work things out. Eliza had to believe that now.

But she'd also come to one other conclusion last night.

It had taken a three-hour-long conversation with Nicole sparked with honesty and courage, enough for her to face a real truth: Eliza had never felt worthy of love. She'd never felt completely, unconditionally loved by another human being. When Reese offered her that, she'd been too frightened to accept it. She'd found a way to sabotage her marriage, leaving Reese before he might leave her.

As ridiculous as it seemed, Eliza felt the truth of that revelation in her heart. She'd been scared of accepting true love from the one man who deserved her faith and trust.

Eliza was ready to give Reese that, now.

If only he'd accept it and take her back.

But first she had to deal with her brother, Blake. And see if he could put a stop to Trina's hurtful meddling.

Eleven

"Aw, hell," Reese said, glancing at his watch. "It's lunchtime already. And I promised to get you back home before noon today. I've dominated enough of your time."

Leanne smiled and offered more graciously than he deserved, "We had to finish up our work here, Reese. Besides, I don't have any pressing plans in Montana or anywhere else this weekend."

"Unfortunately neither do I." Everywhere he looked in his penthouse suite, he was reminded of Eliza and the night they'd shared here. The passion they'd experienced had blown his mind, but it had been so much more. They'd forged a bond of trust that night. They'd really connected, tearing down all the walls that had separated them. Reese had begun to think that they could put the past behind them and look toward the future.

He couldn't begin to imagine how the manure hit the fan in the Fortune household this morning. After reading the *Tribune*'s society page, he could only stare angrily, seeing the harsh words printed about Eliza, wondering how she was coping with all of this. Protective instincts streamed in. But he couldn't do a damn thing to help her unless she wanted him to. At least the truth was finally out in the open.

"You could go see her," Leanne said softly.

He shook his head. "She won't answer my calls." Besides, how could he possibly convince her that she could trust him? He'd been falsely accused twice now and his pride and ego had taken a hit.

"She'll have a change of heart, Reese."

When a loud knocking resounded against the front door, Leanne glanced at him with a gleam in her eyes. Reese wasn't that much of an optimist. But when he answered the door, the last person he'd expected to find was standing in the doorway, glowered at him. "Garrett?"

Garrett moved past him, took one glance at Leanne settled back against the sofa and turned on Reese again with an arch of his brow. "Am I interrupting?"

"No." Reese shut the door, narrowing his eyes. "What are you doing here? Is something wrong?"

Garrett wore his no-nonsense look, the one Reese recalled from their youth, the kind he would have when he thought he'd been robbed by an umpire's bad call at home plate. "You tell me, big brother."

"Garrett," Reese said, walking past him to take his seat again. "It's been a long couple of days. What do you want?"

Garrett's gaze flowed over Leanne, raking her over from top to bottom, a hot, angry glint in his eyes. "Where are you staying?"

Leanne's pretty brown eyes fluttered. "Where am I...what?"

"Staying. Are you sleeping—"

"Uh, Garrett?" Reese finally understood his brother's appearance here. "Be careful. You wouldn't want to use up the small amount of charm God gave you all at once. I don't think Leanne could take it."

Leanne rose from her seat and glared at Garrett. "Are you insinuating that your brother and I...we..." Clearly livid, Leanne couldn't get the words out. She looked at Reese.

Reese snorted and lifted up from his seat. "Garrett, relax. I asked Leanne to work with me here in Sioux Falls so that I could make amends with my wife. Leanne's room is two floors down."

Garrett's jaw unclenched.

"Didn't you get my message?" Reese asked his brother.

"I thought I did, loud and clear."

And you came running, Reese thought. Well, that was one way to unwittingly force Garrett to make his move with Leanne. "Then you weren't listening hard enough. You know, my wife is sure good at handing out accusations. I'm glad my brother has more sense."

Garrett eyed him for a moment, swallowed down, then nodded.

"Don't explain anything to him, Reese. It's none of his business." Leanne's eyes sharpened on Garrett's.

"Oh, I think it is," Reese offered, scratching his head and wondering why the two people he loved most in the world would think the worst about him. Love, betrayal and years of ruthlessness might have something to do with it.

"In fact, you two deserve some privacy."

When Leanne began to protest, Garrett walked over to face her, a smile teasing his lips. "Reese is right. I'd like to speak with you privately. You deserve an apology. I had no right coming here thinking what I was thinking. It's just that…hell," he confessed, softening his tone, "you make me crazy, Leanne."

"There's that charm coming through again." Reese reached for his coat from the closet.

But Leanne's eyes warmed instantly. "*Crazy?* In a good way?"

Garrett smiled wide. "In a *very* good way."

Reese opened the front door. "I'm going for a walk." And a strong Jack and Coke. Garrett was on his own now, and Reese figured if his brother didn't blow it, Leanne might soon become a permanent member of the Parker clan. Now if he could only figure out what to do about Eliza, both Parker men might find this trip to South Dakota worthwhile.

Eliza took a long, hot shower, taking equal time drying off and primping, then styled her blonde locks into soft shoulder-length waves. She dressed in deep shades of red, a bold color and look for her. But what she hoped to do today with Reese was bolder than anything she'd planned in her life. She donned a crimson double-breasted coat—the retro look reminiscent of the sixties—over a tight-fitting red knit dress, with tall black leather boots adding to the whole package of a woman on a mission.

Hopefully not an impossible one.

First she had to deal with Blake. With the late afternoon sun giving way to gloomy clouds, she headed outside and walked the distance to Skylar's homey little cottage, passing the stables along the way. Her father had been right. Seeing Blake's car outside, she knew Blake was paying a visit to his sister. Unfortunately his visits never seemed to extend to the main house. Blake hadn't felt welcome there, though Eliza had done everything in her power to let him know he was just as much a part of the family as his three older siblings. But Blake and Sky had been born of Trina Watters, and though Nash had tried, he never truly convinced his youngest son that he'd belonged in the Fortune family. Her father had built the cottage for Skylar when she graduated college, hoping to keep her close, enticing her with being near the stables and her beloved horses.

With Blake, it had been different.

There was no enticement that could keep him from the sharp edge of bitterness that seemed to consume him. Case and Creed never helped matters, either. They were always coming down hard on Blake. Today Eliza would try her hand at putting a stop to Trina's meddling. Then she'd be free to deal with her husband. Having her family's blessing helped boost her resolve, but with or without it, Eliza wanted a future with Reese.

Blake was closing the front door to Skylar's home when he spotted her standing by his car. Eliza was glad for the timing. She hated the thought of including Skylar in this. Her younger half sister kept to herself mostly, spending her time caring for the horses. So far, she had been untouched by the family's feuding, and Eliza was happy to keep it that way.

"Blake, do you have a minute? We need to talk."

Blake nodded and glanced back at Skylar's front door with a guarded look. "Not here, though. Let's take a walk."

Obviously he wanted to keep their conversation away from Skylar, too.

"We could go into the main house."

Blake scoffed. "No, thanks." He moved along the winding path that led away from the cottage and the lushly sculpted grounds. Eliza kept pace as they headed toward the stables. Once they were a good distance from the cottage, he asked, "What's on your mind?"

Eliza cut to the chase. "You saw the *Tribune* this morning? I take it your visit with Sky today had something to do with that."

He kept walking but slowed his pace. "I read the article, Eliza."

She stopped her stride as they reached the large white-plank double doors of the stables and gazed up at him. He was tall and lean and just as handsome as the other Fortune men. "It's true. All of it. And I'm sorry for lying to you. I've made amends with Dad. I hope you'll forgive me, too."

"I have a feeling you're not here only to apologize."

Blake had always been so darn serious and to the point. She laid a hand on his arm. From underneath his bulky tan leather jacket, she felt his muscles tense. "You're right. I suspect your mother leaked the news, Blake. She's caused trouble for the family in the past, for Case and Gina and then Max and Diana. It's hurtful and it's got to stop. I don't know how she's doing it other than to think she's been spying on us somehow."

Blake closed his eyes briefly. "Damn it. I know. I'm the one who should be apologizing. She's hurt you now, too. What can I do to help?"

Eliza lifted her lips in a small smile. "Talk to her. Make her see that she's not getting anywhere by all of this. And, Blake, you and Case and Creed shouldn't fight all the time. It's hard on the family to see you at odds. Do you think that you can let go of some of your anger?"

He shrugged and didn't bother with denials. "It's been with me a long time."

"Isn't it time to let it go? We're family. Hurting one another isn't going to solve anything. What your mother is doing is proof of that."

Blake pursed his lips and let go a labored sigh. "I'll think about it."

"Thanks—for letting me apologize and for trying to talk sense into Trina. I want you to know that I don't blame you for any of this. It's not your fa—"

"Damn right it's his fault." Case burst out of the stables abruptly and spoke with vehemence, interrupting their conversation.

"Case." Eliza warned her brother with a long, hard stare. She had to admit he looked menacing, dressed in black from head to toe, grasping a leather riding whip.

"Trina's bad news, Eliza. We all know it. And Blake is just sitting back, watching her hurt us. I've been her victim and now so have you."

"Blake's not to blame," Eliza defended.

Blake set his hand on her arm, his fingers gently digging in. "Don't defend me, Eliza. I don't need it. I don't need one damn thing from the Fortunes."

"Great," Case said with a snarl, tapping the riding crop onto his other hand. "Then why don't you take that damn mother of yours and get out. The farther the better. She'd better not try to pull anything else or—"

"Or what, Case?" Blake's tone became lethal. "Your threats don't scare me."

"It's not a threat, baby *brother*," Case said with disgust. "It's a damn fact."

Eliza stood by, watching her brothers argue, unable to intervene. Neither of the two bullheaded men would listen to her.

"Take your bad-ass threats and shove them, Case." Then Blake cast Eliza a cold look. "You see what I'm up against? Sorry, Eliza. I've had enough."

Blake turned on his heel and headed for his car. Eliza watched him until he revved up his engine and zoomed away, leaving Fortune property in the dust.

Shaking her head, she left Case where he stood, too darn upset to say anything to him.

She only hoped her next stop would go more smoothly. Her life—her happiness—depended on it.

Eliza stood outside the penthouse suite holding her breath and bolstering her courage. No matter what she found on the other side of the door, she thought decidedly, she would speak her mind and let Reese know her true feelings. She might be making a huge mistake, but her gut, her heart and her head, believed differently.

She owed her marriage this much, realizing far too late that she had thrown away too many years of happiness. She had unwittingly shifted Warren's betrayal onto Reese without giving him the benefit of any doubt. She hadn't even entertained the possibility that he'd been faithful, and that clearly hadn't been fair to him. She'd proceeded to remove him from her life, thinking it was better to let him go before he found a reason to dump her. Recently she'd seen the folly in her thinking. She'd never fought for her marriage. She'd never fought for what she truly wanted.

Now it was time for her to make a stand and show the man she'd married what she was made of, inside and out. She'd fight for him tooth and nail, if it came to that. But Eliza hoped it wouldn't. She'd had enough conflict in her life lately, hiding her marriage from her parents and dealing with her ever-feuding family.

She raised her hand to knock on the penthouse door then remembered her key card. Boldly she slipped the card into the slot, opened the door and stepped inside.

She found the same brunette on the sofa, her eyes downcast, scouring over a mass of paperwork that draped from her lap to the sofa cushions, eyeglasses somewhat askew on her nose. The long, dark, flowing locks of hair Eliza had seen last night were now tied back in a tight knot at the back of her head.

"Are you guys back already, finished with your brotherly bonding?" she said without looking up.

"Uh, no," Eliza said, uncomfortably. It was obvious Reese wasn't here.

The woman looked up, righting the glasses on her nose with one delicate slide of her finger. Immediately she gathered the papers onto her lap, then set them aside and smiled. "Oh, Reese will be glad to see you." She stood and, as she approached, put out her hand. "I'm Leanne Finnegan."

Eliza eyed her for only a second before taking her hand. "Eliza Fortune...*Parker*. I'm Reese's wife."

God, it felt so good to say that out loud.

"I know who you are," Leanne said far too confidently, irking Eliza no end. So the woman knew she was Reese's wife and yet Eliza had no idea who this woman was making herself comfortable in Reese's hotel room. "About what you saw last night—"

"Listen, I really don't know who you are and what you're doing with my husband, but I'm here to tell you that I love Reese very much. And if you want him, you're going to have a fight on your hands. You see, I happen to know that he's worth the trouble."

"I agree, and he'll be happy to hear you say that."

"Who the hell do you think you—"

"Eliza?"

She turned at the sound of Reese's deep voice. He stood in the doorway, next to his brother Garrett. Though Garrett was a good-looking man, he didn't compare to Reese. He wore tight jeans and a funky faded T-shirt with an emblem of a bucking bronco, reminding her of the old Reese Parker, the cowboy she fell in love with six years ago. But she knew that the prosperous Montana oilman with the sleek sports cars, fancy penthouse suites and to-die-for new home was the man she loved *now*. The two had become one in her heart. She couldn't separate them. He was who he was. And she loved everything about him.

"Reese?"

"I see you've met Leanne."

Eliza held her breath. And when Reese didn't offer any explanations, she was ready to comment…until Garrett walked over to Leanne and slipped an arm around her waist. "Leanne is our geologist. Been with the company almost from its inception. She's brilliant and hard-working, beautiful and…" he said, staring into Leanne's big warm brown eyes, "my girl."

Eliza swallowed. "Your girl?"

She turned to Reese.

Standing with arms folded, leaning against the door-jamb, he smiled.

Then he pushed away from the door and walked over to Eliza, slipping his arm around her waist possessively. He brought her up against him. The solid wall of his chest felt like granite, strong and unyielding. *Dependable.* And oh, so right. "Sorry, you won't have to fight her for me. She's taken. And so are you."

Eliza gasped. "You heard?"

"Everything, honey."

Eliza's heart beat like a drumroll, thrumming hard and fast against her chest.

Garrett grabbed Leanne's hand. "This time it's your turn for privacy, big brother. I'm taking Leanne home."

Reese nodded, keeping his eyes on Eliza.

"Nice, uh…nice meeting you," Eliza muttered, her head swimming.

But Garrett had already swept Leanne out of the suite.

Once they were alone, Reese bent his head and took her in a long soul-searing kiss.

When Eliza came up for air, she spoke with resolute clarity. "You were never unfaithful to me."

"Never, sweetheart."

Tears misted in her eyes. So much time had been lost. But she could only look to the future now. "I love you, Reese Parker."

He hugged her tight. "So I've heard."

"I've never stopped loving you," she admitted softly, pressing her face into his chest.

"Eliza," he said, pulling her away enough to look deeply into her eyes. "I loved you once, very much. I love you now even more, if that's possible. I came here looking for revenge, but instead I found what's been missing in my life. *You.*"

"Oh, Reese." She sighed with happiness, then spoke clearly and honestly from her heart. "I've made a mess of things. I didn't know how to love or be loved and I didn't understand the full scope of what it meant to trust someone fully. How could I when I didn't have faith in myself? I didn't believe myself worthy of your love. We were so happy and I didn't…trust you."

Reese hugged her tight. "Do you trust me now?"

Eliza nodded. "With my life. I do trust you, Reese."

"Enough to leave your home and family?"

"Yes, oh, yes. I want to be with you. I want us to be together."

He brushed a soft kiss to her forehead. "Then come back to Montana with me. You can start up your own design company if you'd like. And I'll be your first client. I'm officially hiring you to decorate my new home. Make it yours. And mine. Make it *ours*. But first I want you to marry me."

Eliza's mood lightened, and giddy with love, she replied with a soft chuckle, "We're already married, Reese."

"I want a real wedding, with all the trimmings. I want our families and friends there. I want us to renew our vows. Hell, we'll even invite the press so there's no doubt in anyone's mind that we were meant for each other."

"Yes," she said with joy overflowing. "I want that, too. So much, Reese."

"So you'll marry me and do up the house of your dreams?"

"Yes, I accept your proposal. I'll marry you," she answered, lifting a hand to caress his cheek. She allowed Reese's love to pour into her freely now. She would welcome it unconditionally, trust him completely and finally feel worthy to accept his devotion without doubts or fears. This time around, she had enough faith in herself for both of them.

"I'm getting the *man* of my dreams, sweetheart." She rose up to brush her lips with his in a sweet mating and the promise of a wonderful future together. "The house is an added bonus."

* * * * *

Don't miss the next DAKOTA FORTUNES *book.*
Be sure to pick up MISTRESS OF FORTUNE
by Kathie DeNosky, available in April.

Turn the page for a sneak preview of
IF I'D NEVER KNOWN YOUR LOVE
by
Georgia Bockoven

From the brand-new series
Harlequin Everlasting Love
Every great love has a story to tell. ™

One year, five months and four days missing

There's no way for you to know this, Evan, but I haven't written to you for a few months. Actually, it's been almost a year. I had a hard time picking up a pen once more after we paid the second ransom and then received a letter saying it wasn't enough. I was so sure you were coming home that I took the kids along to Bogotá so they could fly home with you and me, something I swore I'd never do. I've fallen in love with Colombia and the people who've opened their hearts to me. But fear is a constant companion when I'm there. I won't ever expose our children to that kind of danger again.

I'm at a loss over what to do anymore, Evan. I've begged and pleaded and thrown temper tantrums with every official I can corner both here and at home. They've been incredibly tolerant and understanding, but in the end as ineffectual as the rest of us.

I try to imagine what your life is like now, what you do every day, what you're wearing, what you eat. I want to believe that the people who have you are misguided yet kind, that they treat you well. It's how I survive day to day. To think of you being mistreated hurts too much. If I picture you locked away somewhere and suffering, a weight descends on me that makes it almost impossible to get out of bed in the morning.

Your captors surely know you by now. They have to recognize what a good man you are. I imagine you working with their children, telling them that you have children, too, showing them the pictures you carry in your wallet. Can't the men who have you understand how much your children miss you? How can it not matter to them?

How can they keep you away from us all this time? Over and over, we've done what they asked. Are they oblivious to the depth of their cruelty? What kind of people are they that they don't care?

I used to keep a calendar beside our bed next to the peach rose you picked for me before you left. Every night I marked another day, counting how many you'd been gone. I don't do that any longer. I don't want to be reminded of all the days we'll never get back.

When I can't sleep at night, I tell you about my day. I imagine you hearing me and smiling over the details that make up my life now. I never tell you how defeated I feel at moments or how hard I work to hide it from everyone for fear they will see it as a reason to stop believing you are coming home to us.

And I couldn't tell you about the lump I found in my breast and how difficult it was going through all the tests without you here to lean on. The lump was benign—the process reaching that diagnosis utterly terrifying. I couldn't stop thinking about what would happen to Shelly and Jason if something happened to me.

We need you to come home.

I'm worn down with missing you.

I'm going to read this tomorrow and will probably tear it up or burn it in the fireplace. I don't want you to get the idea I ever doubted what I was doing to free you or thought the work a burden. I would gladly spend the rest of my life at it, even if, in the end, we only had one day together.

You are my life, Evan.

I will love you forever.

* * * * *

Romantic
SUSPENSE

Excitement, danger and passion guaranteed!

USA TODAY bestselling author
Marie Ferrarella
is back with the second installment in her popular miniseries, *The Doctors Pulaski: Medicine just got more interesting...* DIAGNOSIS: DANGER is on sale April 2007 from Silhouette® Romantic Suspense (formerly Silhouette Intimate Moments).

Look for it wherever you buy books!

HARLEQUIN®

Blaze

Discover the power of body language
as Harlequin Blaze goes international
with the new miniseries
LUST IN TRANSLATION!

This April, reader-favorite Jamie Sobrato
takes us to Italy in search of the
perfect lover in

SEX AS A SECOND LANGUAGE

Look for more
LUST IN TRANSLATION
books from Nancy Warren in June 2007
and Kate Hoffmann in August 2007!

REQUEST YOUR FREE BOOKS!

2 FREE NOVELS
PLUS 2
FREE GIFTS!

Passionate, Powerful, Provocative!

SDES07

Silhouette®

Desire

Introducing talented new author

TESSA RADLEY

*making her Silhouette Desire debut
this April with*

BLACK WIDOW BRIDE

Book #1794
Available in April 2007.

Wealthy Damon Asteriades had no choice but to
force Rebecca Grainger back to his family's estate—
despite his vow to keep away from her seductive
charms. But being so close to the woman society once
dubbed the Black Widow Bride had him aching to
claim her as his own...at any cost.

On sale April from Silhouette Desire!

**Available wherever books are sold,
including most bookstores, supermarkets,
discount stores and drugstores.**

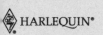

COMING NEXT MONTH

#1789 MISTRESS OF FORTUNE—Kathie DeNosky
Dakota Fortunes
A casino magnate seeks revenge on his family by seducing his brother's stunning companion and daring her to become Fortune's mistress.

#1790 BLACKHAWK'S AFFAIR—Barbara McCauley
Secrets!
What's a woman to do when she comes face-to-face with the man who broke her heart years before…and realizes he's still her husband?

#1791 HER FORBIDDEN FIANCÉE—Christie Ridgway
Millionaire of the Month
He'd been mistaken for his identical twin before—but now his estranged sibling's lovely fiancée believes he's the man she wants to sleep with.

#1792 THE ROYAL WEDDING NIGHT—Day Leclaire
The Royals
Deceived at the altar, a prince sleeps with the wrong bride. But after sharing the royal wedding night with his mystery woman, nothing will stop him from discovering who she really is.

#1793 THE BILLIONAIRE'S BIDDING—Barbara Dunlop
A hotel heiress vows to save her family's business from financial ruin at any cost. Then she discovers the price is marrying her enemy.

#1794 BLACK WIDOW BRIDE—Tessa Radley
He despised her. He desired her. And the billionaire was just desperate enough to blackmail her back into his life.

SDCNM0307